What they said about
BAKED ALASKA AND OTHER STORIES, by Daniel Hoyt Daniels

I liked the prose style – easy to read, and the plots evolved smoothly. The use of words was carefully chosen and concise. The variety made each one stand out by itself. I especially enjoyed reading Baked Alaska, You took the Words, My Brother-in-Law Is a Jerk, and A Few More Days. Each touched me in a different way. Marie in A Few More Days is a wonderful character. On finishing each of these stories, I had a warm feeling.

Your bitterness in the war stories did not surprise me. The tragic ending of each of them made me think and feel the pain of the protagonists. They were extremely well written."
    -- The Hon. Irving Tragen, former US Ambassador Panama, La Jolla, CA

Quite a few chuckles. You write very well and get the reader's attention right away, and your endings are wonderful. You are also able to write from a woman's point of view, like in "A New Start." "The Rabbit" is great! Reminds me of my time in South Carolina when I volunteered in a school there. I really enjoyed reading these stories.
    -- Ingrid Lander, Longmont, CO

Your book is delightful. We especially liked "Happy Thanksgiving"* and "John Harvard Fantoma." "Bastille Day" has everything: nostalgia, youth, politics, sex, humor, and history.
    -- Miriam Mauzerall, Dobbs Ferry, NY

My guests liked it too.
    -- Tinica Mather, Silver Spring, MD

I like your style.
    -- Nancy Myers, Beaufort, SC

I am savoring your stories   I chuckle to myself every time I think of "My Brother-in-Law is a Jerk." Thank you so much. I have ordered some copies through Amazon for Christmas presents.
    -- Coleman Nee, Yarmouthport, MA.

We read your stories with pleasure; we especially liked "Turkey in the Straw,."
    -- Henry and Lois Ross, Nokesville, VA

---

* Note: "Happy Thanksgiving" is to be found in the present volume,

i

ii

Thirty more of the

BEST

SHORT STORIES

of
DANIEL HOYT DANIELS

author of

"BAKED ALASKA
AND OTHER
SHORT SHORT STORIES"

with
Whimsy, Humor, and Tongue-in-Cheek

for your
Guestroom Bedside Table

iii

This book may be purchased at Amazon.com, PDFLibrary.com, and all other online outlets.

Digital Scanning and Publishing is a leader in the electronic republication of historical books and documents. We publish many of our titles as eBooks, paperback and hardcover editions. DSI is committed to bringing many traditional and well-known books back to life, retaining the look and feel of the original work.

Tradepaper Edition 10-digit ISBN: 1-58218-864-5
Tradepaper Edition 13-digit ISBN: 978-1-58218-864-5
Ebook Edition 10-digit ISBN: 1-58218-849-1
Ebook Edition 13-digit ISBN: 978-1-58218-849-2

First DSI Printing: March 2012

Published by Digital Scanning Inc. Scituate, MA 02066
781-545-2100 http://www.Digitalscanning.com and
http://www.PDFLibrary.com

Preface

These little stories are all fictional works originally written for the amusement and pleasure of the author and his friends. Most of them are completely imaginary, although some of them may have originated from a seed of truth. They can usually be read aloud in ten or fifteen minutes, which is the approximate amount of time allotted to each participant attending the periodic meetings of the Beaufort (South Carolina) Writers' Group, under the helpful guidance and encouragement of Ethard Van Stee, the organizer and stylish director of the group. The stories are all unrelated to one another. If the same name appears in more than one story, it is not to be implied that it is the same character. The stories are not arranged in any particular order, and appear approximately as they were written chronologically.

I would like to thank various friends and colleagues for their helpful suggestions. You know who you are. Any errors are of course my own. Comments on these pieces, or requests for reproduction or other use of them, will be welcomed by the author.

Daniel Hoyt Daniels
P. O. Box 1681
Beaufort, SC 29901
March, 2012

"THIRTY OF THE BEST SHORT STORIES"

A Scoundrel, My Father

My father was a scoundrel. A despicable scoundrel, although I was eighteen years old before I learned what a scoundrel he was.

Growing up, I was a momma's boy. I hate to admit it, but it's the truth. I was never very strong, and I was skinny. Oh my, was I skinny. I was Skinny Jimmy, the 97-pound weakling in the Charles Atlas ads. In fact, I didn't even hit 97 until I was 12 years old. Five feet three and 97 pounds.

My father, George, was just the opposite. I mean, he was strong. Beefy, but strong. He could pick up a refrigerator. When we got the new one, he picked up the old one and took it out to make room, then picked up the new one and put it in place. The only thing I could do that he couldn't do was run. I could outrun him like a breeze. And a lucky thing it was too, for I got away from a good many beatings by running. Ignoring, of course, his shouts that my ultimate punishment would be doubled.

I wasn't a bad kid. Maybe not real good, but not bad either. I think my father enjoyed whipping me. He didn't get along with my mother too well, and when she irritated him beyond his normally low threshold he took it out on me, always finding or inventing some reason, something I did that I shouldn't have done, or something I didn't do but should have done. There was no health in me, as far as he

1

was concerned. But I loved Mom dearly, and she was my savior. I don't know how many times she came to my rescue -- came between my father and me when he had me in his sights, and saved me from another whipping. Until I was twelve years old.

Then when I was twelve, Mom died. Thirty-seven years old, she was. Died of leukemia, according to the death certificate signed by our family doctor, who just happened to be my father's brother. I knew she had been ill for two or three years before that. Even as a kid I could notice that she was going downhill. Gradually. Inexorably. But I was eighteen before I figured out the real cause of her death.

The first two years after she died were the most miserable time of my life. I would invent any excuse I could to stay out of the house when my father was home. I usually attributed my absences to school activities or workout at the gymnasium, something my father had always wanted me to do, and which I despised but accepted willingly for the additional time it gave me away from him when he was at home.

A second big change come into my life when I was fourteen. My father married another woman, or maybe I should say she married him. Her name was Raquel. I knew that my father had had other love affairs, and he had even had them when Mom was alive. I tried to tell Mom once. She gently confronted him with it; he of course positively denied it, and naturally I caught a hell of a whipping for opening my mouth. So from then on I kept my trap shut.

2

I had no feeling, positive or negative, about Raquel; I didn't know her at all. In fact, even though I still loved my departed real Mom dearly, I was perfectly happy with the thought of having a new mother and especially someone to get some of the pressure from my father off my back.

The next four years went much better for me. Better because I was more or less ignored in the new household. The other two devoted their attention to themselves, and that was fine as far as I was concerned.

But by the time I was eighteen and a senior in high school, some remarkable things began to happen that changed my life completely. I had never really thought about money in the family. I mean, big money. My father gave me a paltry allowance that I was able to enhance by working at part-time jobs from time to time. He always seemed to have plenty of money himself though, and, although he was just a salesman for a soap company, he had enough to buy his own airplane -- a classic 1959 restored Beech V-tail Bonanza. Said he might need it for work, but as far as I know all he ever used it for was to take his new wife on weekend trips to Palm Beach or one of his villas in the Bahamas. Places like that. I was always so glad to see them leave that I never thought any more about it.

But one weekend when they were gone I found a couple of things of particular interest while poking around where I wasn't supposed to be. The first was a copy of my grandfather's will listing the assets he would leave to my mother. Very sizable assets. VERY sizable. Assets that my father had of course inherited on my mother's death. My father had never spoken of this, but it began to explain some things.

The other thing I found was even more appalling. I think I mentioned that my father worked for a soap company. Actually it was a pretty good sized chemical company and sold, not only soap, but also pharmaceuticals, pesticides, and herbicides as well. Big quantities. Well, I found a sheet of paper that had been folded up and stuck between the pages of one of his books on pesticides. The title of the book was "Pesticides and Their Chemical Composition," and the paper stuck in the book was a copy of an article written by none other than Sir Arthur Conan Doyle, of "Sherlock Holmes" fame. The article was entitled, "Common Poisons and Their Common Usage in Common Crime."

Coincidence? Perhaps, who could say? Gripped by a sudden interest in chemicals and herbicides, I read on. The first poison given in the Conan Doyle article was arsenic. I had heard of arsenic and knew it was a poison. And I had heard tales of people using it to kill. A little shiver ran up my spine as I continued reading.

"Scoundrels bent on evil intent," it said, "customarily administer arsenic in the food or drink of the intended victim in tiny, almost imperceptible amounts, over a relatively long period of time. Arsenic, once assimilated into the body's organs, never leaves. It slowly collects and builds up, and the deleterious effect is gradual and cumulative, often taking two or three years before culminating in a lingering death. Symptoms consist of debilitation and failure of the liver, kidneys, and other internal organs, and are similar to symptoms associated with numerous other diseases. Consequently the true cause

4

of an arsenic death may often go undetected without specific autopsy examination."

Lingering death! My God! That was my mother! All of this describes my mother exactly! My father's a son-of-a-bitch...! Well, I knew that, but I never would have thought he'd KILL someone! My father's a murderer! And Raquel too. They are both murderers!

Call the Police? What for? My father's the smoothest talker east of the Mississippi, with his glib salesman's tongue. It's how he got his job, it's how he gets his women, it's how he got Mom in the first place, and it's how he got her dead! That glib voice of his! Police would never believe me. Not now. Not six years later. Besides, there's no chance for an autopsy; Mom was cremated. Father said that's what she would have wanted. Father said so. And her ashes were spread over the ocean, as Mother wanted, so he said! Yeah! He knew just what she wanted!

Although I was almost blinded by horror and rage at what I had now learned, I dug a little deeper though this stack of forbidden papers, and one more startling piece of information came before my eyes. It appeared that Raquel had been a clerk in the brokerage firm that handled Mom's financial holdings and even had her initials on some of the accounting statements -- going back as much as four years before Mom died.

The picture was emerging in my mind. This woman, who knew the details of Mom's financial condition, contrived to meet my father and turn her wily charms on him, at least three years before Mom's death. Three years!

That's about the length of time it might take for a gentle dosage of arsenic to complete its evil work. She met my father and talked him into killing Mom so she could have him! And Mom's money!

My head swam with the realization of the truth that was now unveiled before me. My rage knew no bounds. I was ready to lie in wait for my father and step-mother and kill them with a butcher knife on their return from their trip to Nassau.

It was only later I realized that if I had killed my father my step-mother would have been the winner; she would have inherited all the money that my father had gotten from my mother! And then if I killed her too, it would be her family that got the money, not me. But I wasn't thinking all that clearly. I am not a schemer, and anything like scheming was far beyond my ability at that point anyway.

I was so mad I had no thought or care about myself. It was not a matter that I considered. I would get them! I would get even, whatever it took. If I had to slip away and go hide in Mexico or Peru for the rest of my life, fine. If they got me and sentenced me to death, that was okay too; I didn't care. In truth, I didn't even think about what might happen to me. I could only think of getting even with Raquel and my father somehow. Any way at all -- I just had to get them. I had nothing else on my mind; could think of nothing else.

Especially I had to get her. She was the one who first set her eyes on my mother's inheritance, and she was the one who planned the whole thing -- my mother's death --

I'll bet. The thought of her killing my mother made me see red.

Tonight they were coming back from their latest trip to the Bahamas. I would go to bed as usual and get a little sleep if I could, then get up at three or four o'clock and do the deed. But, as I began to think a little bit, I realized that a butcher knife might not be the best way to take care of two people. One, perhaps, but not two, and then I remembered the shotgun over the mantelpiece. Double barrel, one barrel for each of them. That's what it would have to be. The death penalty for two murders cannot be any worse than the death penalty for one murder.

They were due back in the evening, so I went straight home after school to lie in wait. I went in the front door as usual, and was surprised to hear Raquel's voice from upstairs, "That you, Jimmy?" It turned out that they had come back a few hours early because Dad had received a call about some urgent business and had gone straight to the office.

However, just the sound of my step-mother's voice re-ignited my fury and I was seized with a sudden pounding tension throughout my body. I could feel the blood come to my temples, and when I shut my eyes I could see the image of her poisoning my mother, her greedy scheme to confiscate the family fortune, and I went into an uncontrolled rage. It was like looking into a blazing red furnace. In retrospect, I can understand what is meant by the temporary insanity you hear about in detective stories and courtroom dramas sometimes. It described me exactly.

I went into the living room and grabbed the shotgun hanging over the mantle that my father and I had used on several occasions to try and make a man of me by shooting clay pigeons. Later these shooting expeditions were significant in court, because they explained my finger prints all over the gun along with my father's.

I took the shotgun upstairs, went into her bedroom, and let her have it, both barrels.

Both barrels. Why not. She collapsed in a heap. I was no longer thinking; certainly I had no thought of what might happen to me when the authorities learned of what I had done. For a moment I couldn't move. It is as though I were watching a movie; it didn't seem real. I must have gone into some sort of shock. The starch drained from my body and I couldn't think. But still, I didn't care. Somehow I did manage to put the gun back on its rack over the fireplace, although I don't remember doing it. I stumbled out of the house, got into my car and started driving, just driving, anyplace.

Where to go? What to do? I had no idea. I had to talk to someone. I even thought of going directly to the police and telling them what had happened, because I knew they would get me eventually. However, I didn't like the idea of leaving my father untouched; if I were going to be leaving this life, as now I knew I would be, at least I would like to take that son-of-a-bitch with me. I would have to figure out how to get him too, but I couldn't think at all rationally in my present state of mind.

The only person I could speak to was Phillip, my step-mother's cousin, who lived just a couple of miles from us. He used to play catch with me sometimes, when I was younger. I certainly wasn't in condition to confront my father; furthermore, my will to kill him was also fading as my knees got weaker and weaker.

I stopped the car in front of Phillip's house. I went up and opened the door without knocking, and stumbled on in. He was in the study. "You look terrible, he said. "What's happened to you?"

"Something frightful," I replied. "Raquel's been shot. In the bedroom, over at the house." I don't know why I didn't just tell him I had shot her. It wasn't as though I were trying to hide anything -- it was more like I was a spectator to something that was happening out there, out beyond me, something that I wasn't even a part of.

"You'd better come in and have a drink. You look terrible," he repeated. "Now, what are you talking about?"

"Raquel's been shot. It was horrible. She's dead."

Phillip's neck and face gradually turned pink, then scarlet, more with rage than with grief it seemed, as my words began to sink in. "No, not Raquel!" he gasped. "Not my Raquel!" Then, biting his lip, he blasted out, "I guess that son-of-a-bitchin' father of yours found out."

"Found out? Found out what?"

"Found out about her affair. Son of a bitch."

"Her affair?"

"Her affair. Raquel has been carrying on an affair for the last two years, and George must have found out."

"And you never said anything? How did you learn of her affair anyway?"

"Personal knowledge... Don't worry," he said, as he tried to cool down and see the picture. "You can stay here and I'll report it to the police. I already understand exactly what happened."

Well, as Phillip understood it or visualized it, my father learned of Raquel's infidelity and coolly and calmly took the shotgun, went into her bedroom, and blasted away. Her infidelity was a clear motive which Phillip presented to the police and all the authorities. He told them who he was and how he fitted in, which was pretty good proof. He explained that he himself was the one who had been having the affair with Raquel, his own cousin, and that he truly loved her. Why he got mixed up with her, I'll never know. He told me later that he always knew she was "bad news," but that he "couldn't help it." Anyway, he got it into his head that my father must have found out about the affair and shot Raquel to get back at her.

Naturally Phillip was nervous about his own safety as well, for he believed that my father would be coming after him next. Therefore he told the police everything, all about his involvement, and convinced the District Attorney and the judge and the jury that it was indeed my father that had shot Raquel because of her infidelity. The fact that my prints were also on the gun was not surprising because, as I may have told you, I had used it for skeet-shooting with my father on several occasions when he was trying to make a man out of me, as Phillip and others could testify.

George was convicted of premeditated murder in the first degree, and, as we live in Texas, a state that embraces capital punishment, he was sentenced to death and was executed on the 15th of November last year.

So, that's about the end of the story.

Now if you will excuse me, I have to go pick up my girlfriend. We are flying down to the Bahamas in my classic 1959 restored Beech V-tail Bonanza for a weekend at one of my villas in Hopetown.

THE END

Sorry, I'm Busy

I was always kind of shy growing up. Around women, that is. I was late in life getting to "know them," to use the biblical term, and the first one I ever knew, carnally that is, was at the beach one summer when I was almost twenty. And that only happened because this doll -- I think her name was Charlene -- found me and decided she had to have me, not because I am all that great, or good looking, or a muscle man, but because she had been stood up by her boyfriend and was mad and wanted to get back at him and I was available. So even though I wasn't in love with her or anything, and had never even seen her before, I did help her get back at him, so to speak. I have to admit that our night together was pleasant, even enjoyable, even superb, even out-of-this-world gorgeous, to put it mildly. So this is what all the poets and French novelists and song-writers and porno artists have been talking about. Wow! I need some more of this, I thought. And wouldn't it be super nice if some day it could be with a woman that I was also in love with!

Now I had never really been in love, not in a romantic sense, although there had certainly been some special women in my life that I had admired, respected, and even adored, but the thought of actually getting into bed with them and doing things to them either hadn't occurred to me or didn't seem right. Up to then. I mean, why would you want to do things to someone you admired and respected?

13

Well, all that changed when I had my first taste of honey, and for several months after that first blossom all I could think of was how to assuage the newly acquired sweet tooth and the craving that had rapidly deployed throughout my suddenly mature body.

Then it happened. It was at the library when I was doing some research for a paper on seventeenth-century French drama that I saw Marie again. Marie was the girl who had lived right next door to us for several years while I was growing up. She was a couple of years younger than I, and the last time I had seen her she couldn't have been more than thirteen, because her figure was just beginning to start budding at the time. Now, however, I noticed that it was in full bloom; busting out all over was the metaphor that came to mind. I had always liked Marie when we were children, and it seemed like a storybook happening that she and I should meet again and find we had so much in common in the way of adult inclinations as well. At least, my inclinations. So I started dating her, because I had the conviction that here was a woman whom I knew I liked a lot, and whom I knew I could love a lot, and who had just as much in the way of physical attributes as the girl on the beach who had first opened the doors to the Elysian Fields of joy and ecstasy for me. I realized my task would be to try and work up to the point of seducing Marie and finding out whether she could be as delightful a nocturnal companion as Charlene had been, or whether what I had so briefly experienced that one time was a unique aberration of nature.

Instinctively I knew I had to take it slow with Marie. I didn't want to spoil things by coming on too fast and scaring her away. I felt growing in me a double sort of love for her -- old love resting on the affection and friendship and adoration I had had for her when we were children, and new love based on romance and physical urges related to the exciting new world that Charlene, my beach doll, had introduced me to. Both things coming together would be a miracle, but here they were, both things in one person, Marie. Potentially, at least. I even had visions of marrying her and living a long and fulfilling life with her, happily ever after, with lots of children.

I thought of different things to do with her, different places to take her, concerts, boat rides, restaurants, walks in the woods or on the beach, suppers at home, cocktails with friends. I was comfortable with her, but compared with Charlene, my progress was... well... awfully slow. I had never yet gone so far as to actually tell her I loved her, but by now I certainly must have given her an inkling.

It was at a polo match one Sunday afternoon that Marie and I ran into an old high-school friend of mine, George Morrison, who was with an extremely pretty young woman, tall and slim, that I had never met before. Betty Thorpe was her name. She was a dancer. I thought dancers were supposed to be short, but I guess there are exceptions to everything. Anyway, it was fun seeing George again, and we had lots to talk about from old times. Furthermore, I was delighted to notice that the two girls, or women as they prefer to be called nowadays, were hitting it off as well.

So after the polo match the four of us all decided to go on to dinner somewhere together, and the conversation continued, pleasantly animated throughout the evening, between old friends and new friends. Marie was quite sparkling and I was proud of her as she was so friendly toward George, and also seemed to connect easily with Betty. The two women were soon whispering, almost into each other's ear, secrets of girl talk, I suppose. How nice, I thought, that she is able to get along so well with other people that way, right off the bat. George liked Marie too; I could see it in his eyes because sometimes when I was talking to him he seemed to be looking THROUGH me, or over my shoulder a little -- looking at Marie, who wasn't bad looking herself, in case I never told you.

As I was taking Marie home she spoke of what a pleasant time she had had that day, with the polo game and the dinner and my nice friends and everything. Especially my nice friends, and how she would like to see them again sometime. So I had the comfortable feeling that I might have made some more progress in my quest to capture her heart and soul and body. I felt that, knowing and liking my friends, she must like me a little more too.

Then a couple of days later I called Marie up and asked her to go to a play with me the following Saturday, a reprise of "My Fair Lady."

"Can't do it," she said.

"Can't do it...? What's happened, is anything wrong?"

"No, nothing's wrong," she answered gently. "It's just that I'm busy Saturday."

"Well, how about Sunday, then? There's a Sunday matinée at 2:00 o'clock. Would that be better?"

"No, I can't do it. I told you I can't do it."

"You said you can't do it Saturday."

"Well, I can't do it Sunday either. I'm sorry. I'll be busy Sunday too."

"Busy?"

"Yes, busy. I'm trying to tell you I'm busy this weekend."

"The whole weekend?"

"Yes, the whole weekend. A weekend isn't very long."

"What are you doing, to be so busy?"

She dropped her voice a bit. "Well, if you must know, I'm going out of town."

"You are?"

"Yes, I am. I think I am falling in love."

Wow! The words hit me like a thunderbolt! Love! Just what I was waiting to hear. I had not yet actually asked her to marry me or even to go to bed with me, but I certainly must have intimated it. So...! She realizes how I feel and has sensed the happiness that my radiant countenance must reveal whenever I am with her.

The image raced through my mind. Well, that's all right. She is going off to be alone for the weekend to gather her thoughts and feelings together... she must be considering a serious life with me! She has to decide in her own mind how she will respond when she hears me ask for her hand! So, maybe she will decide YES, or she wouldn't have to go off by herself to think it through! Yes, it's best that she think it through, as that way she will be sure we are doing the right thing when we get married. Oh yes! And when she really is my wife, I will show her how I can love her both ways, with the admiration and respect we knew when we were young, AND with the romance and passion that is sweeping over us now that we are adults! Oh joy! Oh rapture! Oh, if only I were a poet!

All these thoughts hit me with the speed of light, and, with scarcely a break in the conversation to catch my breath, I asked,

"Well, where are you going for this great weekend?"

"We are going to Saratoga, if that makes any difference."

"WE...? I swallowed hard, almost choking. "Did you say, WE?"

"Yes, the two of us. What's wrong with that?"

"Nothing would be wrong with that, if the 'two of us' were you and me. Marie! I love you!"

There. I said it.

"I like you too. In fact, I'm very fond of you. But this is different."

"So you are going off for the weekend with somebody?"

"Yes, I told you that."

"Well, who are you going with?"

"It all started at the polo match."

"The polo match? Don't tell me you're going off with George...! That Son of a Bitch..."

"No."

"No? Well, what?"

"No... Betty."

THE END

Epilogue

"Betty...?" I sort of stammered, slowly trying to control my surprise.

"Yes, Betty... Have you got anything against Betty?"

"Well, no... I..."

19

"Well, what?"

"No, nothing. Betty's a lovely woman. She's quite gorgeous in fact. It's just that..."

"Yes? Just what?"

"Well, it's... uh..."

"Go on..."

"Can I come too?"

THE FINAL END

Thumbs Up

"It's a boy!" the doctor said. Or the nurse, or the midwife, or somebody there in the hospital. It's what they always say when there is a new arrival, isn't it? Or anyway, about half the time. At least that's what someone always says in the books you read, although in this particular case I was too young to know just who it was that announced the good news. You see, the boy in question was I. So I don't remember the conversation too well, but it probably went something like this:

"Is he healthy?" my mother must have asked. The usual question.

"Yes, it seems to be," one of the nurses answered. In those first few moments of life I was still an "it." It takes a while to become a human being.

"All the fingers and toes and everything there where they ought to be?" -- the second normal question.

"It has ten fingers and ten toes," said the nurse. "But..."

"But what?" my mother asked feebly, still weak from the ordeal.

"But..." said the nurse, "it has ten fingers."

"Perfect," said my mother. "I am so happy."

21

"But, they're not all the same," continued the nurse.

At this point my father joined the conversation. "What are you talking about?" he asked the nurse.

Well, they were talking about my fingers.

I have to interrupt my story for a minute to say that my mother never told me anything about these details of my arrival, and my father didn't tell me until after Mother died, nineteen years later. I was prodding him out of curiosity to explain it to me, and I have tried to reconstruct these early conversations out of what he remembered, not just what I remembered, which was practically nothing, considering how young I was at the time.

You see, although I was born with ten fingers and had one thumb on my left hand, like most other people, I had two thumbs on my right hand like... well, like me. It seems that in the hospital there was quite a little debate about what to do, if anything, with this freak that had suddenly appeared upon the scene, healthy and normal in all respects but one, or should I say three... thumbs, that is.

Mother apparently wanted to cut off one of my thumbs, and the nurse took her side. "Do you want him to have three thumbs like... a freak?" was their argument. We'll just circumcise the second thumb on his right hand. He's so little he won't know anything and it probably won't even hurt him much, like, well, circumcision," they said. Nobody gets the opinion of the patient (or the victim) regarding circumcision anymore. "And," she added, "if we

22

cut off one of his thumbs, he will never miss it: he will never know he had it."

My father and one of the doctors took another view. "Well then, do you want him to have nine fingers, like... a freak?" So, the debate was on.

It seems they finally compromised by agreeing to a minute structural and functional examination of the two thumbs on my right hand to determine, if one of them was to be removed, which one it should be. Often, when unusual things sprout in a human body, like a third tit, they are not really functional, and little would be lost with their removal. If, as some of the doctors suspected, closer examination revealed that one of the thumbs was a useless, poorly connected appendage, it would be removed, leaving the stronger, more normal, thumb free to grow and thrive. The surprise came when the results showed both thumbs fully functional and operational, identical as far as could be determined, and, if one were to be removed, the choice would be a toss-up.

Several more doctors were called in for consultation, while still others heard about this unusual case and, because they knew so little about it, were eager to volunteer their opinions. My father was strongly opposed to gambling of any sort, and accordingly insisted that the process of choosing the appropriate thumb for removal would be just that -- a gamble. Most of the doctors agreed with him, and one of them apparently reminded the other doctors of their mantra to "Do no harm," or, as he put it, "If you don't know what you are doing, better to do nothing." So, that's the way they left it, or left me. Because they did not know what to do, they did nothing. Fortunately.

Frankly, I cannot imagine what life would be like without my two thumbs on my right hand, and when my father related these details of the close call I had had in those early hours of my life, I was sick from picturing the frightful image of what might have been, and at the same time very thankful that I had come out of it all unscathed. It is definitely unfair to scathe children when they are too young to know what is happening to them.

I actually had one less bones than most people. Or, I should say, one fewer bones to be grammatically correct. You are supposed to use the word *less* with quantity and *fewer* with number. That's the school-teacher coming out in me. Interestingly enough, a thumb has only two bones, called phalanges, where other fingers have three, in spite of the greater utility of the thumb. Of course, the thumb's greater utility comes only by way of its unique ability to cooperate with other fingers, or another finger. By itself a thumb is just, well, just a thumb. Being all thumbs would probably be no better than being all fingers -- fingers of the common, three-phalange, variety, that is. My first thumb, or the thumb on the end, can cooperate with any of the three regular fingers, but usually works with the "ring" finger, second from the other end. My second thumb works best with the finger right next to it. It is the middle finger of the five, and it's what I think of as my index finger, but I have to be careful when I hold up a finger to signify "one" to avoid being misunderstood. So usually I hold up my first thumb to mean "one," like they do in Europe. Maybe our European ancestors had two thumbs per hand, for them

24

to have retained the atavistic habit of counting "one" with their thumb (so as to avoid the unintended signal which could be sent by an index finger in the third position).

The first glimmer I ever had that things were different, and by that I mean realizing that my left hand and my right hand were different, must have been when I was still a baby. I know that I preferred my right hand over my left hand when it came to sucking something, and it was my right hand that I held to my face as I went to sleep. My second thumb on my right hand was my thumb of choice for sucking. That was because I could suck it and gently caress the underside of my chin, at the same time, with the other thumb. Of course, thumb number one had its advantage too, because when I sucked that one I could stick thumb number two up one of my nostrils -- either nostril -- but especially the one on the right, because it was more in line. And that was a very pleasant and comforting sensation too -- for a baby, you understand. But still, as a regular routine I preferred the arrangement whereby I could caress the bottom of my chin with the first thumb while gently sucking the second one. I didn't actually suck it, but held the tip next to my upper gum and the soft pad of my thumb, where your fingerprint is -- that part -- against my upper lip. I think I must have been weaned prematurely to have had these drives and to have such a lasting memory of my early oral-digital inclinations.

I remember the first time I ever ate in a Chinese restaurant. I was only about nine, and was with my uncle, who had lived in China, and loved everything about the Chinese, even their food. As we were going into the restaurant, he said, "You know, the Chinese eat with chopsticks; they are a little bit tricky to use at first, but I'll show you how to use them."

Well, I could understand how it might be somewhat clumsy to use chopsticks with your left hand, where you only had one thumb, but if you held them in your right hand, like I did, it was as easy as duck soup, so to speak. I held each stick firmly in two places with a thumb and a finger, and there was, as they say in today's vernacular, no problem. It crossed my mind that the ancestors of today's Chinese also must have had two thumbs per hand, like the prehistoric Europeans, to have invented such a manner of eating. Needless to say, I was immediately better at handling the chopsticks than my uncle was, with all of his experience, but I tried not to show off or rub it in.

I could have been a great criminal or identity thief, for I always had a choice of thumb-print whenever it was required for a license or ID card or anything like that. I could have had an alias with his own identity, and could have proved it. But I am an honest man and I wouldn't want to tell you anything that wasn't absolutely true.

Growing up, when we were old enough to start comparing body parts, I was the most popular kid in the neighborhood. They laughed at first, but then were envious when I showed them some of the things I could do with my right hand that they couldn't do with their right hand, or left hand either.

For instance, when we got to grade school I could shoot rubber bands with one hand, and roll the best spit-balls you ever threw, with one hand yet. I could ring the bell on a bicycle without taking my grip off the handlebar. In Sunday school, when they let us take turns passing the plate, I could hold it with one hand, without a tremor. And I usually needed only one hand to open the screw top of one of those little plastic water bottles we carried to school with our lunch. In chemistry lab in high school I could take the cork out of a test-tube and put it back with one hand. Later on in life I realized other people needed two hands even to use a piece of dental floss or to hold a pair of binoculars while adjusting the focus, things that I take for granted because they are easy for me to do with one hand as long as it is the right one. My right hand, that is.

And something else. Two of my friends always had trouble telling left from right; some people are like that. You tell them to take a left turn and they take a right turn. Well, I never had that trouble; I could always tell.

Guitars were popular among the kids when I was in high school, and one of my friends let me strum his one day. And some of those guys who had accused me of being weird really changed their tune, in a manner of speaking, when I showed them what I could do on the guitar. I mean, I used two picks and could pluck two strings at the same time with the picks. After that they thought I was pretty cool. To me it seemed as though guitars must have been designed to be played with two picks in your right hand. The guys that could only hold one pick seemed handicapped. And, speaking of music, when Carmen Miranda's Cuban style was popular in the 40's and 50's, I got a pair of castanets, and found I could play them both with one hand – my right hand of course -- while simultaneously playing my mouth organ, which I held with my left hand. I don't do that much anymore; I admit it was rather childish.

But besides the guitar and rubber bands and spitballs, I was also a stand-out with the girls. With one hand I could caress them as no one else ever did. I could even pinch them twice at the same time in two different places, if they weren't too far apart.

Everybody is the center of his own little universe, and by that I mean that one's own self is usually one's standard. If you are five feet ten and you live in a country where most of the men are around five six, you think of them as being short. You don't think of yourself as being tall. If you think of skin at all, you think of your own skin color as being normal. Other people are pale, or swarthy, or light or dark, but always in comparison to you. You are the standard. In this country we think of the color of hair as being blond, or brunette, or maybe "brownette," or black or red. In a Swedish passport there used to be a place to check hair color; the choices were light blond, blond, dark blond, and other. We see the world from where we stand. If you like calves' liver and know other people who don't, they are the odd ones, not you. To me, having three thumbs seems very normal. I am normal. I am me.

When, as a young child, I first noticed that my right and left hands were different, I wondered why I didn't have two thumbs on my left hand too. However, I soon got used to having just one left thumb, although two thumbs on the right hand seemed natural.

There wasn't much that "ordinary" people could do that I couldn't do. I even took some violin lessons when I was young, before I ever picked up a guitar, and remember thinking it was a good thing it was my right hand that had the two thumbs. It was easy to hold the bow, and besides, two thumbs on my left hand would not have worked very well, leaving only three fingers on the strings above the finger board. I guess I would have had to learn to play left handed. I saw a left-handed violinist play once -- really weird looking. Think of how different violins might be now if Stradivarius had had three or four thumbs. Or even if he had just been left-handed.

But all in all, I can't imagine life without a right hand with two thumbs. I have told that to doctors and psychologists and curious people and organizations that have even asked me for interviews on the matter. I should think it would be obvious to anybody. Well, I guess you can get used to anything, even having only one thumb on each hand.

So, that's my background. Now I am grown, married with wife and two children, all healthy, with six thumbs distributed evenly among the three of them. And I have a good job as vice-president of a small engineering company. Or ONE of the vice-presidents, I should say. There are a lot of vice-presidents in a company like ours, and in fact if you are not the president or a vice president you are just a wage-worker or hired help.

Anyway, at a company policy-planning meeting the other day, the question of opening a new facility in California came up for a vote. It involved a relatively small investment, but projections indicated it could increase our production by 30%. It was a good idea and we needed the expansion, but it was resisted by our overly conservative financial officer and some others, including the vice president for product design, who I think feared a threat from new blood being brought in. I was strongly in favor of it, and so was the president, as it no doubt would have added to his importance and possibly his annual bonus as well.

"I'm all for it," he boomed loudly, pounding his elbows on the table and holding up his two thumbs. "Let's have a vote. All those in favor, thumbs up!" he bellowed. "Those opposed, thumbs down. Mr. Secretary, count the votes."

Whether the president had forgotten about me, or wasn't aware that I was a freak, I never knew. What I did know is that it's a good thing I was there. There were ten of us present and voting, and, as you have probably guessed by now, the measure carried 11 to 10 when all the votes had been counted.

THE END

The Faithful Wife

I met her in Bangkok, five years ago come November, and promptly fell in love. I married her three months later, proving I wasn't really the confirmed 32-year-old bachelor dandy I was reputed to be. No, she wasn't even pregnant and I had no gentlemanly obligation whatsoever to marry her, even though I must admit it all happened pretty fast, fast enough to make some people -- people with dirty minds that is -- wonder. No, she was quite virginal, to my knowledge, although her virtue, if we have to call it that, was certainly not the result of any decision on my part to exercise restraint. It was a condition that was quite out of my hands, something that, until we were married the following February, I simply hadn't been able to do anything about, in spite of the efforts I devoted to the cause.

Excuse me, but I think I should back up and clarify something. To be precise, that November was not our very first meeting, for I had seen her briefly in Paris four years earlier. At that time, I was to be found in the City of Lights engaging in a little fun and diversion while gathering substantive material for a superb novel about the French Revolution, although it was never actually published because of short-sightedness on the part of the editors guarding the doors at Harper and Random-House. But be that as it may, one afternoon, in my unceasing quest for greater learning, I wandered into a lecture hall at the

Sorbonne where the topic of discussion was French influence in Southeast Asia in the Nineteenth Century. The strange thing is that the speaker was Siamese, or Thai as they are called in these modern times; strange because Thailand is one of the few countries in that remote part of the world that never went through the experience of being a colony and, to my knowledge, never was under the domination of a European power. Even China had suffered its British influence and its Opium Wars. Anyway, the discourse was interesting, and also interesting was the attractive young woman I, thoughtfully and carefully, just happened to sit next to, who turned out to be the daughter of the professor giving the talk. Her name was Cali Han, which means Lovely Lily, or something exotic like that, in some obscure language. Unfortunately, Cali Han and her father had already made immutable preparations to depart for Bangkok the following day. Therefore, famous though I am for my prowess with the ladies, I had insufficient time to develop any memorable liaison or interlude such as those quick five-to-seven trysts which the Parisians affectionately call "*cinq-à-sept*." I had to settle for merely opening my little black book and uploading her name to my collection of other potential or imaginary lady-friends. I persuaded her to yield her address as well, explaining that I would like to seek her out (and her father too, of course) if I ever got to Bangkok, never really thinking it likely or even possible.

Well, as you are now aware, not only was it possible, but it came to pass in fact. Four years after my Paris sojourn, I was working in Hanoi as a foreign correspondent for a major US newspaper. At that point I had gone sixteen months without a break, and felt justified in granting myself the uplift a little vacation could offer prior to my return to the States for another assignment. Just about that time, one of my colleagues breezed in after a visit to Bangkok with glowing reports of the beauty and seductive charm of that city. Now I have always admired beauty and seductive charm, so I closed my eyes long enough to imagine the romantic attractions of Thailand, and of course I immediately recalled my delightful meeting with the daughter of the Thai professor years before on that particular occasion in Paris. Picturing the advantages of having a friendly contact in an unknown and exciting metropolis, I forthwith dashed off a three-page letter to Bangkok telling Cali Han how vividly I remembered her, how much I had been thinking about her over the intervening four years, how busy I had been with just no time to write -- please forgive me -- and how I could never forget her, and how sincere was my desire to see her and her pretty face again. I almost embarrassed myself by laying it on so thick, but her social circles seemed unlikely ever to intersect with mine, and the excessive exaggerations of my eloquent language seemed unlikely ever to catch up with me or damage my already somewhat less-than-sterling reputation. So I made my plans, yielding to the vision of exotic ecstasy that awaited me among the Siamese lotus blossoms.

Of course, I was not sure that Cali Han would ever receive my letter; her address might possibly have changed, or she might have left Thailand and gone to live in France or some other distant land. Fortunately I had the foresight to allow myself sufficient time for two or three exchanges of correspondence before setting out on my quest for a final fling at oriental happiness. Her first reply arrived in just one week, and naturally my juices if not my heart almost overflowed with delight. She did remember me, she said, albeit slightly, and of course would gladly condescend to see me if I were to honor Bangkok with my visit. Although it seemed to me that the intensity of her joy was somewhat mitigated by her adding that the Thais have a reputation for hospitality which she felt she should uphold, I didn't let that detract too much from the spirited anticipation with which I viewed the project. So my foot was in the door, and I rapidly sent her several more well-crafted love notes describing the intensity of my excitement in anticipating our reunion after such a prolonged and arduous separation. Besides, I thought it would be a gentlemanly and chivalrous thing, for me to bring a little happiness into the hum-drum life she must have been leading as a down-trodden translator in a silk-exporting firm. If she tumbled for me, as of course was likely, it would be a memorable learning experience for her that she could cherish all her life. "I'm on my way," I said in my final letter before briskly boarding the Garuda Airlines jumbo jet, Bangkok bound.

My first sight of Cali Han fitted perfectly with the image that my creative imagination had so vividly formed in my inward eye -- the lotus flower in the Garden of Eden. But soon I was a little disappointed, for she seemed reluctant to meet with me and my body in any surroundings that might allow or even suggest the slightest degree of intimacy or impropriety. During the ensuing ten days, she did condescend to meet me several times for lunch in one or another of the many oriental restaurants one finds in Bangkok, but never in the evening and most certainly never overnight. That was strictly no no. One afternoon when the tropical sun was still smiling down on all the straw hats and flowers of that tropical paradise, she took off early from work so we could hike out to see the elephants working in a logging operation on the edge of town. Saturday we went for a boat ride in one of those elongated dugout canoes with an unpronounceable Thai name and an odoriferous outboard motor that sped us through a labyrinth of canals rivaling those of Venice. On other days, after she got off work, we had a couple of visits to museums and pagodas in the late afternoon -- touristy places like that -- and even a visit to the famous Bangkok Zoo. She seemed to enjoy showing me the sights, and the proximity of Bangkok to the earth's equator allows abundant late afternoon sunlight even in November.

There was only one little matter that bothered me besides the fact that she wouldn't spend the evening or the night with me; she never took me home to meet her family. I would have liked to meet her father again, but she told me he died a year ago. "Left this earth," is the way she delicately expressed it.

It soon became all too clear that my macho urges were unlikely to find any physical satisfaction from Cali Han, and under normal circumstances I would have abandoned the endeavor and sought feminine company elsewhere. I had noticed that there always seemed to be a plethora of pulchritudinous young women scattered throughout the Bangkok metropolis in the restaurants and bars everywhere I looked, and I began to wonder what innate stupidity was causing me to limit my attentions to this one woman. In spite of her name, Cali Han remained adamant in her reluctance to let me hold her hand, let alone kiss her or anything. Why waste time with her, I thought, when there are so many other fish in the sea? Then late one evening my clouded vision briefly cleared, and I was astonished by what I saw.

It had been less than a week, and I suddenly realized that I was in love. "How is that possible?" you might ask. And indeed, it is the very question I asked myself. I cannot answer; it made no sense, but there it was. *Voilà.* Love, that mysterious supernatural force I had so often brushed against and always, although sometimes only barely, overcome in the past, was now encroaching on my sense and sensibilities once again. And I surmised that Cali Han was also developing a gradually increasing affection for me, judging from the manner in which she gazed into my eyes and from the way her smile revealed the happiness deep within her heart when she was near me. Her voice resembled that of a daytime nightingale, if such a creature exists. Although I still had not gotten to first base with her in any physical sense, she revealed, to my thirsty eyes, a rare intelligence and understanding, and she radiated a warm potential for compassion and future togetherness.

All this was conjecture, you say, and that may be true, but my image of her had clarified, and by now it had become obvious to me that she was an extreme case of a condition that we used to call "good girl syndrome," which meant, "nothing premarital below the nostrils." She would be a faithful wife; that was quite obvious. She was saving herself and her favors for the right man -- her future lifetime partner.

By the end of the week I was so captivated by her explicit and implicit charms that I could not imagine myself ever cavorting or consorting with anybody else. The many other women I had known in my life had all been relatively easy conquests, as it were. I am not bad looking, if I do say so myself, rather dapper in fact, and I am comfortably off financially. "Financially secure" is the more elegant term, the expression you see in the upscale mix-and-match magazines for lonely singles. I have a tenured sort of position with a well-established firm, I draw a satisfactory remuneration, and I have some modest deposits earning interest in a Merrill Lynch brokerage account. So this exotic Lovely Lily, this Cali Han, with her cool, untouchable beauty, loomed as both a challenge and a prize. I made up my mind to marry her, and was of course delighted when she agreed. I bought her an expensive ring and told her to wait until I could wind up some loose ends of my work in Hanoi, then in a few weeks I would get her a visa and reenter Bangkok like Young Lochinvar out of the West, gather her up, and smartly whisk her off to New York, where we would have a storybook wedding and live happily ever after.

And that's about the way it worked out, We are now married and enjoying comfortable suburban life in a neo-colonial house with a white picket fence in Scarsdale, an easy commute by train to my office in the city. Cali Han has slipped smoothly into the social life of the neighborhood. She loves plants and horticulture and botany and flowers -- that sort of thing -- and is a good gardener, so she is a popular member of the Scarsdale Garden Club. Last year she started offering Thai dancing lessons through our local YWCA and now has 23 budding

Terpsichoreans in her class. She has learned to play a respectable game of tennis and has always been a good swimmer. And she is very good-looking in a bathing suit, I should add, if I have not already said so. Definitely outstanding in all the important points. She has been a good wife to me and a good housekeeper, neither parsimonious nor profligate, if you know what those words mean. I think she has saved most of the earnings from her teaching, which is fine with me, and I would surmise that she may have been squirreling away a portion of the rather generous allowance I always give her for household expenses, but that is all right with me too. She is everything I could want in a woman. She is a dutiful and faithful wife.

We have now been married five years -- five idyllic, happy years. I have been living in heaven, like a dream. It would be hard for me to imagine life any other way, and I don't think Cali Han could readily do it either. At least I didn't think she could until yesterday. Then something happened.

When I came home late from work last evening, Cali Han seemed a little quieter than usual. Her outward manner has always been demure and modest, but this time it was particularly so. She spoke in subdued tones, but nevertheless went right to the point. Orientals have the reputation of maintaining an inscrutable conservatism when there is something important on their minds, but not Cali Han.

I want to go back to Thailand," she said, out of the azure blue.

"Thailand?

"Yes, Thailand."

"All right," I said. "That's fine. No problem. I should have thought about taking you back for a visit long before this."

"I have to go alone."

"Oh...? Well, that's all right, if that's what you really want. How long do you expect to be gone?"

"I'm sorry, I don't think I'll be coming back."

"Not coming back?" I said, stupefied, hardly able to speak.

"My husband is sick, and I have to be with him."

"Your HUSBAND?" I muttered. Or stuttered.

"Yes. We were never divorced, and it's my duty to be with him in his time of need."

"With HIM? What about ME?"

"You'll be all right. You're healthy. And you're financially secure."

And that was that. Cali Han, the faithful wife.

THE END

Oh, Didn't You Know?

It is certainly an interesting phenomenon of the human character how people can change like chameleons depending on surrounding circumstances. I mean, you think you know someone, and then something happens in your life, or in their life, and suddenly you realize you just don't get it. It seems as though you don't, or never did, know them at all.

Take Edie and Lane, for instance.

For reasons I don't need to go into right now, I got married soon after college when I was still wet behind the ears, as they used to say. The thing I will mention, however, is the family I married into.

Let me stop a minute and remind you that when you get married you may be marrying an entire family and not just a nubile maiden they have offered up on a débutante altar. Anyway, the family I married into, the Blair family, largely comprised a bunch of stuffy old coots who nursed their egos on the shrinking remnants of glory left over from the halcyon days of Francis Preston Blair and Montgomery Blair the First, scrambling socialites and aspiring politicians back in the time of Abraham Lincoln.

My wife Janet wasn't even a Blair; it was her mother who was the Blair: a tall, slim, long-nosed Blair by birth, one who had somehow reached down a little from her lofty

41

social position in the nation's capital to marry a prosperous gentleman with the prosaic name of Jackson, but the Blair dye was not to be rinsed out in one or two generations. On all her correspondence, and social invitations with raised engraved printing, my mother-in-law was Ellen Blair Jackson, with the word Blair of course being prominently centered at the letterhead.

Now this Ellen Blair Jackson, having set the tone for our story, no longer figures herein. Our focus turns to her niece, one Edith Blair Staton. Edith's mother was another social battleship, the twin sister of my aforementioned mother-in-law, and her father was a suitably resplendent Admiral of the US Navy. Hence this Edith Blair Staton was first cousin to my dear wife, Janet. Edith, like others in that tribal clan, clung to the Blair element in her full legal name like a limpet sticking to a wet rock in the North Sea, and she made sure that her full name appeared prominently among the lists of "married maidens" in the proper Registers and Blue Books, although within the family she was affectionately known simply as Edie.

Now we shall see how coincidences and unforeseen events can affect people's lives and attitudes, and even influence their relationships with other human beings.

Although I had met Edie and her husband at various weddings and funerals and a few family dinner parties, I would not go so far as to say I knew them very well until Janet and I found ourselves singing in the same choral group with Edie one September. It was the Oratorio Society of Montgomery County, a horrible name, but the music we produced was actually pretty good. Although her husband, Lane, was not a singer, Edie started bringing him to our house for supper occasionally after our Monday evening rehearsals. Lane and I would spend the rest of the evening playing chess or discussing politics and labor problems while the ladies talked of their gardens and children, and maybe even shared some mysterious secrets of girl-talk to which I was never privy. And that went on all winter, until the Society gave its final spring concert. After that, singing rehearsals were suspended for summer vacation, and our suppers with Edie and Lane were suspended too.

And then something happened.

For reasons that I won't go into here, Janet and I got divorced that summer; she went her way and I went mine, but when fall came, and rehearsals began again, I went back to the choral group, which I had always enjoyed. I took my place with the basses and looked around to see who was there from last year. Sure enough, there was Edie in the alto section as always. I would see her at intermission and say hello, I thought.

Well, intermission came, but she had other ideas. I mean, I went up to her, smiled, and said, "Hello, Edie, how have you been?"

No response. Nothing. She continued to look at the wall behind me as though I were invisible. Now, many members of the Blair family had myopia and wore thick glasses. Maybe she didn't see me. No, that couldn't be the problem; myopia is near-sightedness, and I was only three feet in front of her. It must be something else. Maybe she

43

had been carried away to dreamland by the music, or had gone into a thinking mode and was mentally running through the alto part from the last piece we had sung. Yes, that was it, I decided, as I saw her open her mouth and begin to speak to me.

"Oh, Beatrice," she said, "have you seen the latest issue of "House and Garden?"

She was looking right through me and was talking to Beatrice Thornapple, a blond soprano standing ten feet behind me. I was the original Invisible Man.

Well, that continued throughout the whole singing season that year. I tried to give Edie several opportunities to respond to my cheery "Hello's," but to no avail. No response. Zilch. My invisibility surrounded me like a cloud.

Edie wasn't the only member of the Blair clan who gave me the cold shoulder after Janet's and my divorce. They all did: first and foremost my mother-in-law, then her brother, who until then had been a golfing partner of mine. Another was our family doctor, who was a Blair as well. If you can believe it, our dear Dr. Blair even had his office manager transfer our files and refer us to another general practitioner with Blair nowhere in his history. In those days, it was unheard of to sully the Blair family name with a divorce. Shocking. I would learn my lesson. Did learn my lesson.

In due course, another September arrived, time for the choral society to reconvene once again. I went to the opening rehearsal as usual, fully prepared to ignore Edie as she had ignored me, so you can imagine my surprise when she came bursting up to me like a babbling brook flowing out of an Appalachian spring in springtime. "Oh, hello, Dan," she gushed, all smiles and warmth. "How have you been? How was your summer? Bla, bla, bla."

I was, to put it mildly, rather taken aback.

"I've been all right," I politely responded. "Thank you for asking."

At that point the music director called us to our places. I re-directed my concentration back to Vivaldi and Buxtehude. It was clear I would never understand women, this one or any other. Had she changed, or was it me? Was I imagining things, or what?

At intermission time she came briskly up to me again and we picked up on some more inconsequential conversation. Then I asked naïvely, "And how is Lane?"

"Oh, didn't you know? We were divorced last month. He's living in California."

THE END

45

The Telegram

It was three a.m. on a quiet Sunday morning when there came a loud pounding on the bedroom door and an excited voice called out, "Señor Gómez! Señor Gómez! There's been another *coup d'etat*! Another *golpe de estado*!

"Caramba" was the word that dominated the murky thoughts of Juan Gómez as he dragged himself out of a sound sleep, lifted his heavy eyelids, and began to realize the ominous portent of this unwelcome news.

Three a.m. Sunday in Japan meant Saturday noon in Central America. Gómez was his country's Consul in Osaka, having been appointed by his friend, President Alfredo Vallegas, only two years earlier, not long after Vallegas assumed the presidency. Gómez's position, as one of his country's senior diplomats, was now suddenly in jeopardy.

"Who's taken over control this time?" Gómez asked his excited deputy.

"It's the three colonels again, Sir, the same ones that put Vallegas into power in the first place. What are you going to do?"

"We have to recognize facts," said Gómez. "Go draft a nice congratulatory telegram along the lines of the one we sent Vallegas after *he* took over. It should still be in the files."

47

So, with little editing and much haste, Gómez signed and shot off an appropriate telegram welcoming the triumvirate of colonels into power and wishing them every success in all their future endeavors.

Now, the president of that little Central American country, Alfredo Vallegas, just being ousted, had a reputation for being a good man, very intelligent and sincere, but he didn't have much formal education. He was a man of the people, although he himself had come to power by a forceful takeover known as a *golpe de estado*, or *coup d'état*. We democratically-inclined Americans, here in the United States, overtly frown upon any *coup* anywhere, unless of course it happens to put a man in office who is someone of our own choosing. In Vallegas's country there had been five such coups and only one presidential election in the previous 18 years, not a very good record.

Although Vallegas came into power by a *coup*, he stressed in all of his public speeches how devoted he was to the cause of social justice, economic development, and help for the poor. He had previously served with a certain degree of distinction in the National Guard, and his takeover had been supported by three Colonels named Sanjur, Silvero, and Nentzen, who naturally had expected to strengthen their own position by having their friend Vallegas in the presidency.

As it turned out, the colonels benefited somewhat less than they had hoped. However, Vallegas's ambitious social reform program was very popular among the masses of the people. Its targets were widely publicized and included a certain amount of land redistribution, improved health care, increased primary education, and an overhaul of the financial system, which had been dominated by foreign offshore banking interests.

The United States was naturally worried about this course of events, tending as it clearly did toward Socialism and possibly even Communism, and its obvious threat to our national security. To add to our concern over this, Vallegas was believed to be strengthening his diplomatic and commercial ties with several other countries known to have leftist-leaning governments, including Cuba, Venezuela, and Trinidad.

Our Central Intelligence Agency, the CIA, was charged with monitoring the activities of Vallegas's government, and thwarting policies and practices that might be inimical to our hemispheric interests. Fortunately, having sufficient "black bag" funds, which did not have to be accounted for, the CIA was able to enlist all three of the aforementioned colonels on its payroll to provide intelligence on the activities of Vallegas and other government officials. For instance, when it was learned that Vallegas was considering levying a tariff on fruit being exported to the United States, the CIA was able to take the necessary steps to block such an action because of the effect it would have on the profits of a major US corporation.

Shortly after that affair, it was decided in Washington that Vallegas would have to go, although he had been in power less than three years . The CIA turned again to the three colonels, who were proving quite loyal to us, and found them very willing to plan and carry out another coup, for they now foresaw an even greater increase in their own power and influence with Vallegas out of there. They would take over as a triumvirate and rule the nation. They anticipated little opposition; such coups occurred frequently, and were almost accepted as normal.

The colonels and their cohorts timed their plans to seize the president's office one weekend when Vallegas was out of the country, visiting in Mexico. They swiftly took control of the TV and radio stations and government buildings, and sealed off the harbors and airports as well as all border-crossing points, preventing the possibility of Vallegas's return until they had consolidated their position. The curfew that weekend affected all the country's marinas and yachting facilities, deep sea fishing operations, hiking and rock-climbing expeditions, sky-diving ventures, and tourism establishments that ran special jungle excursions for bird watchers from the Audubon Society of North America.

Special editions of the national newspapers, and radio and TV broadcasts, announced the change of government, and a flood of congratulatory calls and telegrams started pouring in from friends of the colonels' and sudden sympathizers of the new government. One of the first people sending a congratulatory telegram was Señor Juan Gómez, the Consul whom Vallegas had appointed to serve in Osaka, Japan, and who now was understandably concerned for his job and the continuity of his diplomatic career under the new regime.

But that's not the end of the story. It seems that Vallegas had a friend who owned a small private plane, and, with the cooperation of faithful followers back home, Vallegas was able to sneak back into the country under the radar and land on the beach in the light of automobile headlights which had been lined up by his supporters eager to keep him in power.

Once back in the country, Vallegas called upon loyal elements still serving in the National Guard, and, within 48 hours of the abortive coup, he was back in power. The curfew was lifted. The three colonels and other perpetrators of the attempted takeover were jailed for two months until the CIA clandestinely freed them.

And oh, one more thing. Señor Gómez now had to fire off another telegram from his post in Osaka to his government back home, 48 hours after the first one. This time his telegram came straight to the point. It read:

CANCEL PREVIOUS TELEGRAM – GÓMEZ

THE END

Thirty of the Best Short Stories

The Last Word

My wife Sally always had to have the last word. Women are sometimes like that. I don't mean that all women have to have the last word; that would be an uncalled-for sexist thing to say; even I realize that. And I'm not talking about women in general. I am talking about Sally, my wife. My ex-wife, to be exact. Or is it "former wife," like "former president," if you have had two? Anyway, she always had to have the last word. Always. It was not just about important decisions, like what kind of a car we should buy or who should we ask for dinner, or whether we should send more troops to Afghanistan. I'll give you an example:

Sally would argue that grapefruit juice was better for you than orange juice because orange juice had too much sugar in it and sugar was bad for you. "I like orange juice," I would say. But what we had for breakfast was grapefruit juice. She saw to that. It was her way of getting the last word. Like being one up on me.

Or we'd have a discussion on politics. Our political views were often even more different than our stances on fruit juice. I remember talking with her about some newspaper reports of corruption in the United Nations. "We should just get out of the UN," she would say. I held that the UN did a lot of good and that we should strengthen it and pay more attention to the positions and interests of

53

other countries. "That's just because you went to Harvard."
I rolled my eyes around, but I couldn't argue with that,
because it was true. She had to have the last word, and that
ended the conversation.

"All right, all right," I would agree. "Whatever you
say." Then I would put my arms around her and try to kiss
her to show how much I loved her. She backed away.
"You're only saying that because you're feeling horny."
Again, the last word. Undeniable. You see, almost
invariably her last word would be naked truth -- hard to
refute.

So our marriage had its ups and downs. I guess all
marriages do, in their own way, and ours did for sure. I
really did love Sally though, certainly more than anybody
else I have ever known. She was an intriguing person,
intense internally, but with the external appearance of
controlled calm. I think she loved me too, although it took
her some years to accept the fact that I was not as rich as
she had initially assumed or as I had possibly implied
during my dashing courtship days.

I never made much money. She wanted more. My
work for the Government required frequent travel and
extended stays in far-off places all around the world, so the
possibility of her holding a nine-to-five job and also being
with me was out of the question. I admit that it might have
been a hard decision, for her, to choose between me and all
the money she could have made if she herself were working
at a good steady job back in the USA. As she saw it, the
choice was me or money. I was glad she chose me, but she

often reminded me that the choice had been difficult. "If you would only settle down in one place," she sometimes said, "then maybe I could get a job too... "

It wasn't as though she couldn't have had a job while following me around: she was a pretty good writer and had even published a few stories and some poetry when she was younger. She also had a degree in music and, if she had really wanted to, could have given piano lessons practically anywhere, not to mention English lessons in most of the foreign countries I worked in.

Although the jobs she could have had were plentiful, even if low-paying, she had never gotten engaged in any kind of remunerative work, in spite of her talk. I think she felt that, if she did not hold a job with a salary equal to or greater than mine, any other work would be menial and beneath her. If she wasn't one-up, it wouldn't do. As a result, I had to be careful to see that she wasn't overwhelmed with too much free time on her hands, even when we lived in interesting cities like The Hague, Sao Paulo, and Stockholm.

The good works and charities and ladies' clubs that I helped her get into did soak up some of her energy and seemed to satisfy her when we were living in those places, and even for a time in England, where her forebears, of whom she was so proud, originated. (Interesting, isn't it, that we Americans, with our Constitution eschewing anything smacking of nobility, are so fascinated by the lives of British aristocracy and royalty, and even pay questionable researchers to trace our ancestry back to William the Conqueror or Henry-the-Something-or-Other.)

Anyway, when we came back to stay for a while in the States where things were more familiar to her and the novelty we had known abroad was no longer with us, our differences had more of a chance to surface and somehow we ended in divorce. By then she was well into the habit of not working, and I guess the absence of the exotic diversions overseas resulted in our getting tired of looking at each other's face over the breakfast table here in the USA. People sometimes ask me why we got divorced, and, to tell you the truth, I still don't know exactly why. I guess we just "drifted apart," as they say. But I never felt the animosity toward her that some people I know harbor toward their "ex's." As far as I know there were never any "third parties" involved (perhaps unfortunately, as that might have eased the transition from married bliss to single euphoria.)

Now, I can't really speak for Sally, but over the next few years I didn't find anybody else in particular that I could imagine taking her place in my household and in my life. I did date a few other women, but never met anybody I would want to marry or settle down with. I don't know who Sally had been seeing, but as far as I know she had never remarried or gotten significantly involved with anybody else (understandable, naturally, considering that she had already had the best).

However, after a good many months with her out of my mind, and without further thought on the matter, I ran into her last Sunday evening at a cocktail party and felt something of the old attraction that had gotten me involved with her in the first place, such a long time ago. I suppose I must have unconsciously felt there was a possibility of our

56

getting back together somehow, for, almost without realizing what I was saying, I spontaneously asked if she would have lunch with me the following Thursday. I remember being quite pleased when she smiled and said, "That would be very nice." We set a time, and she chose -- she was the one of course who had to decide -- she chose a nice restaurant downtown. I was to go ahead and make reservations.

Wednesday afternoon I got a call from Sally's brother, Peter. "Is that you John?"

"Yes, what?"

"I am sorry to have to tell you this, but Sally had a heart attack last night."

"Oh my. How's she doing? Was it bad? Is there anything I can do?"

"I'm afraid not. She died before we could get her to the hospital. She only said, 'Tell John I don't think I can make it on Thursday.' It was her last word."

THE END

Divorce, Old French Style

There was a young Prince of France, back in medieval times, whose name was Charles. His brothers were Philippe and Louis, but he was Charles. He got married at a tender age, when he was still in knee-pants. Or rather, "they" married him, at a great big party, to a beautiful child princess he had never seen before. Her name was Blanche de Bourgogne, and she came from Burgundy, which was a separate entity from France in those days. She had been sent from her homeland over to Paris for the occasion.

In those days, most marriages, especially royal marriages, were arranged, as they were matters of national policy, like manifest destiny and colonization, or corporate mergers and acquisitions. The wedding was a piece of elaborate ceremonial cake to bind the cheese and confirm the international accords, but for Charles, at age eleven, it was just like another birthday party.

Even as he got older, Charles was never really into women, if that is the proper expression, and many people believed his childhood marriage was never actually consummated. Perhaps that gave some grounds or justification to the charges of wayward behavior in subsequent years on the part of young Princess Blanche. We do know that Charles favored the outdoor life of hunting and fishing across vales and hills, or jousting and drinking with his male relatives and masculine friends, in preference to hunting and fishing in the bedroom. It was

59

said that, as far as women were concerned, he didn't know which end was up, and was never very interested in finding out. He, like his two younger brothers, was definitely a man's man, even when he reached nineteen.

As history would have it, about that time Charles's two brothers married two beautiful young women who were happy-go-lucky cousins of Blanche's, also from Burgundy. With their love of parties and sparkling social life, the newcomers brought a boost of excitement and joy into Blanche's existence and an uplifting atmosphere of gaiety into the activities of French courtly life of the day -- and the night too, for that matter.

All three of these young ladies loved the excitement of balls and functions and games of charades and blind-man's-bluff and *cache-cache,* especially such games and activities as closely involved the many young gallants always hovering about. They liked to do anything they could to liven up the royal court. However, the three husbands continued to devote their interests and activities to sports and the outdoor life, so much so that they sometimes neglected their fun-loving wives. Accordingly, it is understandable that the poor young ladies might have had to seek attention from other sources, which, fortunately or unfortunately, seemed to be readily available.

When Charles became King on the sudden death of his father, he was reluctant to change his sporting routines, and Blanche, now a queen, saw no need to change her gay way of life either. The couple seemed to get along fine, neither of them paying much attention to the persona or activities of the other. They maintained a reasonable exterior façade but, in truth, they more or less ignored each other.

One day while still in his early 20's, King Charles got a report from his Minister of Inside Information to the effect that he, the king, was losing popularity with the populace, who thought his lifestyle too frivolous and self centered. Seeing this as a challenge, Charles was suddenly inspired to make a name for himself and gain some glory laud and honor from his Christian subjects. Accordingly, he promptly organized a Crusade and set off toward the lone and level sands of the East, to slay the infidel Saracen and perhaps even try to recover the Holy Grail.

Some members of his entourage were personally devoted to the King; others, faithful followers they would be, went along in hopes of gaining points or kudos when the time came to call the roll up yonder. An effort to clear their sinful slates, as it were. However, the farthest they got was Carthage, on the coast of Africa near present-day Tunis, where the gleaming cohorts of their adversaries surprised Charles and came down upon him like the wolf on the fold. Charles and his men were unable to breast the wave and suffered one defeat after another. Finally, wounded, sore bestead, and realizing they would be unable to save their heroic cause, they gave up the chase and collected their decimated remains for the return to Paris, with their tails between their legs and bitter frustration in their heavy hearts.

It was this frustration that led to Charles's depression and possibly a touch of mental derangement. He dreaded the reception to be expected in Paris and became almost psychotic on the matter, although that term was not yet in general use in those days. He feared that men would think him weak and ineffectual; women would begin to believe the insidious old rumors questioning his manhood. Life would be miserable. To make it worse, even while out of the country, he continued to hear talk about his wife's behavior back in Paris, and he began to give credence to tales he had previously ignored.

When he did get back to Paris, frustrated in spirit and weary in body, his wife Blanche greeted him with a warm hug and welcoming suggestions, which he interpreted as being her way of mocking him or hiding some aspect of her own questionable activities. And, because he needed some object toward which to vent his spleen, he took it out on her, letting himself believe the ever-increasing talk about her naughty behavior while he was away on God's mission.

In his agitated state of mind, Charles became the very victim of own his thoughts and fears. As he thought, so was he, you might say. He imagined that his head ached, so he had headaches. As he convinced himself, rightly or wrongly, that Blanche had been having adulterous affairs, he began to feel the horns of the cuckold sprout upon his brow, which now was wet, no longer with honest sweat, but with the righteous wrath of a man who had been wrongfully wronged.

Now there was never any proof of wrongdoing, but there certainly was a lot of smoke in some of the furnaces round about. Things such as visiting cavaliers in the palace leaving the beds in their assigned quarters un-slept in, and appearing for the morning hunt weary and bleary eyed; articles of clothing turning up in boudoirs not one's own -- things like that. Of course the servants knew what was going on, but, unlike today, when servants blab forth everything they hear, there used to be a code of conduct regarding rumors. Servants were not supposed to repeat intimate conversations they had overheard, and if they did, no one was supposed to believe them or pay them any attention.

It's not that Charles was really worried about his standing in the eyes of Blanche and her cluster of noble ladies. It was an irrational fury, coupled with his concern about his image in the eyes of other people around the royal court, men that is, for no man likes to have his buddies think him a wimp. His fighting blood had been brought to a boil by the African sun, and the climate he found on his return to Paris was insufficiently soothing to calm him down. So with frenetic fury he forthwith charged Blanche with adultery and had her imprisoned in the infamous Château Galliard Dungeon.

As if that were not enough, and to purge his court of the appearance of all sullying influences, he let his wrath continue to rage, and he similarly slapped her two sisters-in-law into another horrible prison on similar charges. After his disastrous half-baked crusade against the Infidel, Charles was no longer a man who would settle for doing things half way, or even two thirds of the way. In his fury he had to lock up all three of the naughty girls.

Now with his wife and her cohorts adequately disposed of, Charles could stop worrying about the appearance of his conjugal bedroom and start living again, devoting his energies back to his old familiar occupations. Having caught his breath, he now started sending his armed forces to fight against easier targets, like deviant little frontier villages or groups of nobles who had gotten uppity in his absence or had not yet been fully integrated within his own domain.

Thus, King Charles regained a semblance of control over his affairs, personal and official. Some years went by.

In due course, the king's advisers in the Privy Council told him he should get himself another wife to bring back some elegance and tradition to the court. They also fondly hoped he might possibly produce a future male heir to the throne so as to prevent the extinction of the Capétien royal family line. Charles was amenable.

There was only one problem: he still had a wife, out of the limelight though she was. What to do with her? Poison or hanging were not good options this late in the game, for they would be all too obvious and might cause an unacceptable drop in the king's popularity polls, which for years had already been under considerable downward pressure. More sellers than buyers, as it were. Furthermore, like many devout Christians of the day, Charles believed in life after death. A heavenly paradise, he feared, might ironically turn out to be a pleasant reward for his wife's wayward behavior rather than punishment for her earthy earthly sins. To assassinate Blanche might be doing her a favor. Sort of the Oh-Death-Where-Is-Thy-Sting attitude.

Divorce seemed the only means. Recalling that it was Pope John XXII who had married them, for better or for worse as it were, Charles went through the proper channels and asked the Pope for a divorce, only to be told that there were insufficient grounds. Adultery was not nice, the Pope agreed, but if the Church started throwing stones now, stones would soon be flying all over France and the entire Christian world, and, before long, there might be no stone left unturned, a thought that caused even the Pope to shudder.

Charles thanked the Pope for his polite explanation and accordingly made a generous monetary contribution to the Vatican coffers to express his gratitude and appreciation. Nevertheless, he went on hoping that some positive solution could be found. Discouraged but not disheartened, he continued his entreaties, and asked again, "Are you sure nothing can be done?"

"Well, let's see," said the Pope this time, trying to be helpful and realizing the upside financial potential of some insider trading with the King of France.

Therefore, it was only a short while later that the Pope's emissary came to King Charles and announced that extensive research at the Vatican's Division of Genealogical Archives had revealed Charles and his wife Blanche to be consanguineously related, being seventh cousins once removed. Since incestuous marriages of any blood relatives were forbidden by the Church, all the Pope could do would be to annul the marriage. "Would that be all right?"

Charles thought it over for a nanosecond or two before gently replying, "Well, yes. That would do just fine."

And so it came to pass. The marriage was annulled. Charles felt a new burst of freedom. He was so delighted to be free of Blanche that to show his thankfulness and generous spirit he had her punishment downgraded from a life sentence in the dungeon of the Galliard Château to a life sentence in the Convent of Maubisson Abbey, where the walls were only ten feet high and bread and wine were served every morning.

Free at last to find himself a proper wife, Charles sent out his emissaries to all the neighboring kingdoms to find for him an appropriate young woman of royal blood to be Queen of France -- hopefully a more suitable and more dutiful wife this time around.

But Blanche was like some women who, if you give them an inch, will take a mile. Better though life in the convent was, she wanted more. She only learned of her marriage annulment through the convent grapevine but promptly began to lay her plans. Although she was still not supposed to have contact with the outside world, by bribing some of the Mothers at the nunnery she was able to enlist the services of a famous lawyer, well versed in theological law and matters of intrigue. The man had previously achieved renown though his brilliant defense of a priest scandalously accused of seventeen incidents of child-molestation.

Blanche told her lawyer what to do, how to prepare the legal case that she wanted to bring to court, and exactly what damages she expected to collect.

The case did go to court, and, given the sordid popular interest in the details of any litigation smacking of scandal, the authorities expedited it through the system to get it out of the public eye as quickly as possible. Fortunately, it came at a time when the volatile French political pendulum had swung a bit toward the side of Liberté and Liberalism. In just six months the case was brought to a close, and the High Tribunal Court of Paris decided Blanche's case against the Government in her favor. The principal points in its decision, after an introduction of lengthy legalese, read essentially as follows:

In the case before this court, involving Blanche de Bourgogne versus King Charles and the Government of the Kingdom of France -- bla bla bla -- this tribunal, being duly constituted and altogether fitting and proper -- bla bla bla --

has duly and truly determined that:

ONE: Charles Capet, now King Charles IV of France, and Blanche de Bourgogne were married by Pope John XXII in the year 1307.

TWO: In the year 1314 Queen Blanche was convicted of adulterous behavior and sentenced to life imprisonment in a maximum security facility, without eligibility for parole.

THREE: By the decree of Pope John XXII on September 11, 1325, the marriage of Blanche and Charles was annulled.

FOUR: Because of the annulment, she was never married.

FIVE: Because she was never married, she could not have committed adultery.

SIX: Because she could not have committed adultery, her arrest and imprisonment were improper, illegal, and without foundation.

SEVEN: Because her arrest and detention were illegal, she is not a crook and is hereby acquitted and exonerated of all charges and allegations, real or imaginary.

EIGHT: And finally, because of her unjust suffering and forbearing under improper arrest and detention, she is herewith awarded compensatory consideration consisting of lifetime payments in the amount of 50,000 FF French Francs per year to be drawn from the Royal Treasury, and annually adjusted for inflation in accordance with the current cost-of-living index.

Case closed.

THE END

Epilogue

Blanche left Paris and returned to her native land of Burgundy on the Rhône River and soon joined up with an old friend, the Duke of Savoy, one of the first men she had ever known, so to speak. The Duke was a charming but impoverished nobleman who was her second cousin on her

mother's side. They were married in a non-religious cere-
mony, with lots of friends and admirers cheering them on.
Because the laws of the Catholic Church against incestuous
marriage were still in effect, they had to forgo the big
church wedding and settle for the services of the local
magistrate or Justice of the Peace, or whatever they called
him in those days. They lived happily ever after that; she
was reasonably faithful to him and had lots of children,
many of whom were apparently sired by the Duke himself.

THE FINAL END

White Man in a Black Skin

I can remember, when I was a young child, some of the things my mother used to say about blacks, or colored people. "Darkies" was the affectionate term she often used, alhough you wouldn't say that now. Being from Alabama, she was of course an expert on race and race relations. It wasn't hard for me to learn at an early age that the offspring of a mixed marriage between a white person and a colored person was always colored. I remember asking my mother (step-mother she was, actually) why this was so, and her answer made it clear very quickly: "It's because black blood is stronger." But I soon learned we were not just talking about African blood.

When, in my late teens, I went to study for a semester in Mexico City, I noticed that the students had skin color of every shade from light tan to deep brown, but a few of them were as white as any Swedish milkmaid, and they weren't foreigners: they were Mexicans of Spanish descent. And the professors were almost invariably light skinned. It was the same thing in business and government: the higher the position, the lighter the skin color of the person, as a general rule. Later on, I also found this to be true in France and other countries, as it certainly was true in the United States. Herrenstein and Murray, in their controversial book THE BELL CURVE, related economic success and career success in the United States to race and IQ, but it was not just the African blood that seemed to be tinting or tainting people's genes and pulling

71

them down. In India the caste system is directly related to skin color. And they're Caucasian, dark skinned though most of them are. Jawaharlal Nehru, a Brahman of the highest caste, had a light skin color that US Ambassador Chester Bowles once described as that of a gently cultivated Florida winter suntan. In fact, in India the native name for "caste" signifies "color." Down the scale, people were darker and darker, and blackest of all were the Untouchables, with rare exceptions. But most of the interest and focus on race and position and intelligence seemed to be right here in the United States.

Whether all of this scaling was racial prejudice, or whether some of it could possibly reflect any basic racial differences in reasoning or cognitive ability, such as IQ, was something I wondered about, but it was almost a taboo subject. I thought then, and still do, that the difference was the result of upbringing. When I read Herrenstein's book, I became quite concerned. Although I don't think this book was an attempt to prove that blacks were mentally inferior, it did cite undeniable statistics showing blacks in general did not score so well on so-called IQ tests. At one time I wondered whether mulattoes, or those who had partly black blood and partly white blood, would have average IQ scores that were between those of pure blacks and pure whites, but I have never seen statistics on that question, and it certainly would have been a touchy subject to investigate.

Later on, arguments or discussions on these matters came to be known as the "nature versus nurture" controversy. In other words, aside from any cultural bias that IQ tests might have had, was the apparent correlation between race and IQ the result of upbringing and environment, or innate ability and genetic makeup? Or could it be accounted for by cultural bias in the tests?

As luck would have it, my chance to find out began when I was 24 years old. I was teaching in a boys' school in Pennsylvania, and my wife had had a miscarriage with complications that forbade her ever having children. Although one never sees his own prejudices as others see them, I do not believe that either of us was prejudiced racially. We decided to adopt a baby, and when we learned that the teen-aged black girlfriend of the janitor right on campus was pregnant with a child she did not want, we arranged for an adoption.

The child turned out to be a healthy boy, and it didn't take us long to forget about his skin color almost entirely. He was our child, and we raised him as we would have raised the child we lost, giving him the greatest love, and education, and training in social behavior, of which we were capable. We gave him our name, which is Schwartzkopf; he was Jimmy Schwartzkopf. In school he was generally in the upper half of his class, mostly B's, a few A's, only occasional C's -- not the outstanding student we had hoped for, but above average. He even got a partial scholarship and entered a liberal New England college, where, to my amusement, they wanted to know if he planned to become Jewish. Another Sammy Davis Jr., I guess. Remember, this was quite a while ago; I don't think they proselytize like that anymore.

But Jimmy didn't like his life at college very much. He liked English, studied journalism, and was a pretty good writer (for which I think I can take a lot of credit), but his relations with the other students were varied. One portion of the mostly white student body seemed to accept him, although Jimmy never knew whether it was because they felt it was their duty to do so, or because they really liked him and admired his personality and abilities. Another portion of the whiteys seemed to ignore him as though he carried a cloud of body odor about his person. They were not overtly impolite to him, but just paid him little or no attention, almost shunning him, as though he weren't there. The few other black students on the campus had little to do with him either, viewing him as being uppity or trying to act white, and I can't help thinking they felt that way because we had taught Jimmy to speak correct English with a good vocabulary and proper pronunciation.

We were pleased when Jimmy graduated number 87 in his class of 350, although we had hoped he might make *phi beta kappa* or at least *cum laude*. We had some satisfaction from the fact that he had the highest academic standing of any black in his class, and I was quite comfortable knowing we had given him the best upbringing and education possible to enable him to succeed in the competitive world which historically has been so dominated by whites. He would be a success in whatever endeavor he undertook, of that I was sure, although I could not have answered the question of which of the two forces -- nature, his own innate talents; or nurture, the loving and attentive upbringing we had given him -- was the foremost reason for his success, but that was no longer a matter of concern to us.

I did feel that, after the somewhat awkward and not-too-happy time Jimmy had had in college, when he got out into the real world and his upbringing and true ability had a chance to show their stuff, he would have a very happy life with a great deal of success both financially and socially.

74

Jimmy was well qualified for any work involving journalism, writing, or literature of any sort. He was a good writer, a logical thinker, and an articulate speaker, I am proud to say.

After graduation, when it was time to look for a job, Jimmy knew he wanted to work in what the schools call "communications," namely radio or television. Scanning the job opportunities being offered, he learned that the people at a small radio station in Richmond, Virginia were advertising for a number-two announcer to back up their anchorman. Jimmy immediately set his heart on becoming a radio announcer.

Now, all of this was happening back in the days when integration efforts were the strongest, and companies and corporations and institutions were under pressure to establish some reasonable racial balance in the makeup of their personnel. Over the years my wife and I had almost forgotten about our son's race, but we knew he should be a shoo-in for any job he sought, what with his superior education, upbringing, and minority class membership to boot.

So Jimmy filled out the necessary application forms for the radio announcer job, and drafted a superb covering letter, terse and coherent, describing his interest and qualifications for the job, and sent it on in. He was staying with us in Pennsylvania at the time, and was ready to drive to Richmond for an interview had they so wished. The next week they called him and said they were interested, and would like to ask him a few questions. Did he mind being interviewed on the telephone?

No, of course he didn't mind. After all, it was his voice that they were going to be using if he got the job; it was understandable that they wanted to hear his voice. Jimmy and his mother and I were proud of Jimmy's speaking ability and his use of the English language, and we knew he could only impress the radio station people.

So, after their discussion on the phone, they said they would be back in touch with him.

He waited two weeks, confident that he had made a good impression and hoping to have a letter of acceptance, telling him what the conditions of his employment would be and when to report for work.

He did not get the expected letter, but got another phone call from a Mr. Richard Whitehead, the radio station personnel manager. Whitehead apologized for not writing, saying the matter might be too delicate to be put to paper.

"Too delicate?" said Jimmy. "I don't understand."

"I am sorry, Mr. Schwartzkopf. You have many outstanding attributes, but I regret to say we cannot accept your application."

"Would you mind telling me why? I thought I had all the qualifications you were seeking for the job."

"Well, that's the delicate thing, Sir. In the current atmosphere, we are under restraints to maintain a certain racial balance in the composition of our personnel."

"All right... "

"What it means, Mr. Schwartzkopf," he said, lowering his voice even on the telephone, "is that we have decided we need to hire a black man for the position."

"That's fine. I'm black."

"You are? Well, you don't sound like it. I'm sorry."

THE END

COMMENT: I wrote this fictitious tale because some years ago I saw an article about a black doctor who was having trouble getting patients. According to the article, when the doctor was a baby he was adopted by a professor of psychology who was a do-gooder and civil rights activist. The professor had a very high IQ and adopted the African-American baby with the idea of proving he could develop it into a genius in a mostly white society. This was in the early days of the nature-nurture debate, and at that time there were many people who were concerned regarding the consistently lower scores of blacks on standardized measures of cognitive ability, known as IQ tests. The professor wanted to prove, or at least test, his belief that IQ is culturally acquired rather than inherited genetically. As I recall that article, the experiment didn't turn out too well.

The young black fellow, with all his education and erudition, found himself isolated from his black cultural roots, and for a time while growing up he was not only frustrated but even suicidal. In his visits to various black communities he was accused of putting on airs and of being an "Uncle Tom." The adoptive parents of the black boy thought they were doing him a favor by giving him a superb education and bringing him up "white." But it turned out to be no favor at all. The child, then youth, then young man, was miserable outside of the classroom, never fit in, had no significant social associations other than by mail with people who did not know his race. (Wouldn't it be interesting, I remember thinking at the time, if political candidates could campaign without appearing in photographs or on TV so the color of their skin would be unknown? Their ethnic origins could then be surmised only by their voices.) The tale went on to tell how the black fellow easily sailed through medical school at the top of his class, interned for a time at a big city hospital, and then set up his own practice in a small Southern black community which he felt most needed his services.

To his dismay, and what the point of article was, the black patients there preferred white doctors. They did not want to go to him because they thought he probably had benefited from reverse discrimination through Affirmative Action, and feared he might not have been bright enough to get into medical school on his own. That's what the article said. But maybe the writer had his own prejudices.

THE FINAL END

A Hallowe'en Ghost Story

This story is true, and you can believe it or not. We were seven years old, my brother and I – we are twins – and it was the first Hallowe'en that we were allowed to go trick-or-treating without our parents. As long as we stayed right in our own neighborhood.

It was a pretty big deal to us, almost like getting your driver's license when you are sixteen. We didn't believe in ghosts or witches or any of those things, or so we thought, but we did believe in candy and cookies. So we took our black and orange bags with us and set off down the street collecting goodies. We had to be home by 6:30, but by then our bags were full. It was just getting dark when we went back to our house. We weren't supposed to have any candy until after supper, so we wanted to eat early.

We went into the house but there was nobody there. Then all the lights went out, and we heard a spooky voice coming from outside, going WHO... WHO... WHO...! By now it was really dark. We were sitting in the living room and didn't know what to do. We didn't even have a flashlight, so it was pretty spooky. Then there came a knock on the door. Three knocks: BOOM... BOOM... BOOM...

I opened the door a crack and saw this ghost standing there, and that's the truth. Making this WHO... WHO...

79

sound. I slammed the door shut and had to go to the bathroom because I had wet my pants. It was pitch dark there in the house, but I was able to grope my way back to the toilet.

Just then the lights came on and I heard Dad's voice call out, "Billy and Johnny, are you there?" Well, that is one time I was really glad to see my Dad, but then he started laughing, and Mom came up from the cellar and was laughing too.

The ghost was Dad dressed up in a sheet to scare us, and Mom had gone down to the basement to make it worse by turning off the lights at the master switch.

My Dad is kind of a nut. He then said he would give me and Johnny 25 cents for each piece of candy we had gotten, so I made $36.75 because I had 147 pieces of candy. Johnny made about the same. It was the most money I had ever had in my life.

Then my Dad threw all the candy into the garbage but two pieces of butterscotch for each of us. Dad's a dentist, and said it was bad for our teeth and all that. Then he got a watermelon out of the car and some grapes and bananas, and that's what we had for dessert. After that we started calling my nutty Dad, "Casper, the Friendly Ghost." What a nut.

THE END

Toothpaste, Anyone ?

She was a big woman, almost as big as I was, sturdy and strong. Sturdy of body and strong of mind. You knew she was strong when you danced with her, like at one of those company functions they used to have back in the days when they did things a little more elegantly than they do now. I mean, she would hold you close, even closer than you wanted. At least, she would me. It got to be sort of embarrassing, especially dancing to the slow stuff. It is harder to push a woman away than it is to pull her toward you. Broad hipped, broad breasted, broad minded, generally speaking a broad broad, you might say. She gave the impression of being a woman who didn't like being said no to, and one that usually got her own way.

My problem was even worse than that of the average guy in this predicament, with a dancing partner trying to pull in too close. You see, the one I was dancing with was Darlene, the wife of my boss, Mr. Bailey. So that meant she was a married woman. And as if that were not bad enough, I had a wife too, so that meant I was a married man. I hadn't even been married very long, but my own wife didn't like to dance. I couldn't help thinking how nice it would have been the other way around -- if my wife had liked to dance and my boss's wife didn't.

But in truth it went deeper than that; it wasn't just dancing that was the problem. Now it may sound as though I am flattering myself or putting on airs, but it's true that I

81

am a pretty good looking guy, at least this Darlene seemed to think so, and she -- well -- wanted me. She had me in her sights. At dinners she sat next to me whenever she could, or across the table from me where she could slip off her shoe and innocently rub my ankle with her toe. Or brush against my arm or shoulder in the hallway or getting in and out of the car. Constantly, things like that. There were a couple of other young men in our office that were almost as good looking as I was, and one of them was even single. Why she couldn't focus on one of them I'll never know.

When I was younger my reputation hadn't always been too good around town, and I had had some affairs and things that I wasn't too proud of, but most of that was before I was married and went to work for the company where Darlene's husband was my boss. However, more recently I have been trying hard to live a moral and upstanding life, hoping to make people such as my in-laws proud of me, so getting involved with the boss's wife just didn't fit in with my career plans at the time. But like I said, she was a strong woman, and I'm sure she had a good deal of influence over her husband, who was a nice enough guy, but in my opinion something of a milquetoast around her. To put it bluntly, she dominated him. Maybe I'm something of a milquetoast too, but at least I resist being dominated my a mere woman who is not my wife, if you can call Darlene, and her muscles, mere. Furthermore, I don't think I have even let my own wife dominate me very much, although she may see it differently. If she does, she is so subtle about it that I don't notice it.

For a long time I tried to ignore Darlene's advances, or to pretend that they were nothing but my imagination or fantasy, on the theory that if you ignore something long enough it will go away. But no, Darlene didn't go away; she hung in there, ubiquitously hanging over my head like the sword of Damocles, dominating my existence like the Matterhorn towering over Zermatt. I sometimes wondered whether other people in the company were aware of her interest in me, as it gradually grew and developed into an inexorable quest for my submission to her control and drove away any doubts I may have harbored regarding her intentions.

Now there is no easier way to lose your wife than by having her find out you have been fooling around with your boss's wife. And an easy way to lose your job is to make the boss's wife mad enough to tell the boss you are a no-good employee that ought to be gotten rid of. My wife or my job? I was between Scylla and Charybdis -- a rock and a hard place, as it were.

I would look around at my colleagues at the office when Darlene was concentrating on me, and wonder what they were thinking. At first it seemed they were always focused on other things, other people, maybe other people's wives, or husbands... who knows? But as the pressure from Darlene kept building up and up, I was afraid I could not go on maintaining a straight appearance of indifference forever. Of course, I feared that, when and if she came to the realization that she was banging her head up against a stone wall, she might take offense and with vindictive malice get back at me through her husband, who controlled my position with the company. What was it that

Shakespeare or somebody said about a woman scorned? I didn't need Hell's fury on top of me. I feared what I thought she could do, and I feared what I *knew* she could do... to me. Maybe I would have to start throwing her some scraps or tidbits to take the keen edge off her appetite, give her a sweet, soothing, brotherly smile if I could conjure one up. Should I calm her with a gentle grin occasionally? Could I do it without arousing her primordial passion even further? What to do? Oh, what to do? To zig or to zag? If I had an affair with her, I might lose my wife. If I didn't have an affair with her and made her mad, I might lose my job.

My wife; that's a thought. Should I enlist my wife's support? I didn't want to open an old can of worms with her about my affairs or relations with other women. Anyway, most of that happened before were married or even knew each other, but when she got into one of her moods she liked to bring up some old moldy adventure of mine, true or not, and throw it in my face. She never really trusted me, whether she had any reason not to trust me or not not to trust me. Usually there was no reason. No reason not to trust me, that is. Usually.

I had been with the company in Pittsburgh seven years by then, had had a couple of promotions, and had moved up to Vice President for Inventory Control. That may not sound like much, but it was probably the most important job in the company, for we made our money buying and selling. Buying big lots cheap and selling small lots expensive. Double or triple or even five times the original price sometimes.

We had to have enough inventory to fill orders promptly to keep up our reputation, but did not want any more inventory than necessary, for that would cost us money in lost interest, not to mention storage expenses. Anyway, I liked my job well enough, and wanted to keep it. With the economic hard times, I had friends that had gotten laid off, and new jobs were hard to find in those days.

We handled all sorts of sundries: hats, dolls, sunglasses, T-shirts — even cigars. Most of these products were made overseas, including of course the cigars, which constituted an important segment of our business and income.

The best cigars were, and still are, made in Cuba, and the best market for them was, and still is, the USA. My company sometimes imported Canadian products like maple-sugar men and wooden cutting boards and fake Eskimo carvings in imitation ivory, so we had the channels set up for imports. It was easy to have cigars imported into Canada and then brought on into the United States. Not exactly legal, perhaps, but not hurting anyone and not breaking any law, strictly speaking, just ignoring a stupid Treasury Department regulation issued by the Bureau of Foreign Assets Control against supporting Castro's economy by spending money in Cuba.

Well, one day my boss decided he had to go to Havana to check on his suppliers, but wanted to minimize any trace of his trip there from the United States. I think he was being overly cautious, but he didn't want to fly from a US airport to Cancun or Nassau or any other obvious jump-off place for Cuba, and he wanted as few people as possible to know about his trip. So he had me drive him to the Toronto

85

airport, a distance of almost 300 miles. All right with me --
I was still getting paid and don't mind driving. Anything to
keep him happy. And keep my job.

But 600 miles round trip was more than I felt like
undertaking in one day, so I booked ahead into the Toronto
Hilton for an overnight before the drive back to Pittsburgh.

I had a little surprise when I picked my boss up at his
home that day, for there Darlene was with him, not kissing
him goodbye, like a dutiful wife, but coming to be with him
on the drive to the airport, like a dutiful wife. There was
nothing I could have said, even if I had had anything to say.

The six-hour trip to Toronto was uneventful. We made
it on time, but even before we got there I started
wondering, and worrying a little -- wondering what I was
going to do with HER. She must have read my mind, for
after we dropped Mr. Bailey off at the airport, she said,
"You're not thinking of driving back to Pittsburgh tonight,
are you?"

"Well, I don't know," I said, "maybe it would be best if
we did head on back now. I could have you home by
midnight." (It was five-thirty then.)

"I thought perhaps you planned to stay the night in
Toronto."

"As a matter of fact, I did, originally. I made a hotel
reservation at the Toronto Hilton, but I can cancel that. If
you cancel before six o'clock there's no charge."

"I guessed you might want to stay over, so I made a reservation too."

"All right. What hotel?"

"The Toronto Hilton."

Now that sort of hit me. How could she have picked the Toronto Hilton, I wondered. I hadn't told anybody I was staying there, and Toronto is a big city with almost three million people and dozens of hotels. But then, the Toronto Hilton was obviously well known. Maybe it was just a coincidence. I'll let it ride, I thought.

I had to take her to supper though. I found a busy restaurant with a lot of light and a lot of people, who might help to keep her from feeling too cozy in case she had any ideas on her mind. Then a movie to fill in the evening. I was getting tired by the time we got back to the hotel, and I hoped she was too.

"I have to go to the Ladies Room – you go on and register," she said. I got assigned room 902, got my key, and politely waited a couple of minutes until she came back out to the registration desk. Then, would you believe, she got room 904. Another coincidence?

Well, I hope there is a room 903, I thought as we were riding up in the elevator. But there wasn't. At least not on our side of the corridor.

The bellboy left our bags with us and said goodnight. I tipped him, said goodnight to Darlene, and we took possession of our respective quarters.

Well, that wasn't so bad after all, I thought. Then when I got inside my room I noticed the connecting door. Locked, of course. The doors were designed so they could be opened to make a sort of suite of the two rooms. Not this time, however. This time they were staying locked.

I washed up, got into my pyjamas, and was just about to crawl into bed for a well-deserved night of dreamless sleep, when I heard something. A light tapping. Tap, tap, tap. No, it wasn't my imagination. It was the inner door.

"Yes?" I said, "Are you all right?"

"I'm fine. Have you got any toothpaste?"

Stupidly, without thinking, I let it pop out, "Sure." Then I realized I had been tricked, but it was too late. She had gotten her foot in the door.

And that was that.

And I have never told anybody else about it, even my wife, and I don't know why I am telling you, except that it's the truth.

But I still have my job at the Company.

THE END

Without My Glasses

I can't see too well without my glasses, you know. One of my wife's duties is always to watch where I might put my glasses down, whenever I take them off to go swimming or take a shower or go to bed. Things like that. So she can find them when I need them.

We had been living in a nice house with a picket fence in the suburbs for about twelve years when a pretty young widow lady moved in next door. A sweet little thing, if I do say so myself. Even a tender morsel wouldn't be an exaggeration. My wife and I tried to act like friendly neighbors toward her. At least I did. No ulterior motives, of course. She would come over occasionally for a drink or a barbecue with some other local friends, and soon we were on a first name basis. Her name was Bianca, which is Italian for Blanche.

So, one evening when my wife was out for her Planned Parenthood meeting, the doorbell rang, and there was this Bianca standing on the porch. Not really unusual; she had rung our doorbell before, although never when my wife was away. But we have always been hospitable, so I asked her in for a drink. No harm in that.

Well, to make a short story short, it turned out that a drink wasn't all she wanted. She wanted company. as well.

Preferably masculine company. She insisted I sit by her on the couch, which was all right by me. Then a whiff of her delicate Chanel perfume wafted over me. I felt the touch of her hand on my forearm. I felt the ineffable sensuality of her half-closed eyelids and the inviting beauty of her half-opened lips. And I felt for a moment that I was no longer in control of my actions or my destiny.

Then, distracted as I was, somehow I must have dropped my glasses, just as her tender breath caressed the lobe of my right ear. "Kiss me, my Handsome Hunk," she said.

How could I refuse? She had me where she wanted me.

But oh, the sweetness of those lips! I hadn't tasted anything like that since I had my first chocolate-caramel upside-down cake at the Chevy Chase Hot Shoppe when I was a freshman in high school. I... was... in... Heaven.

Then something happened.

The front door burst open and there was my wife, frozen in horror at the panorama she was beholding. "What do you think you are doing there kissing Bianca?" she stammered.

"Bianca... ? I thought it was you I was kissing, Honey. You know I can't see too well without my glasses."

THE END

Run, Run !

Have you ever had that dream where you have to run because you are chasing someone or someone is chasing you, but your feet are in a quagmire or a swamp and are sticking every time you try to pick them up and make them move? You try as hard as you can to run, but all you can do is painfully slog along at the speed of a slow walk. It is horrible frustration.

Well, I used to have that dream occasionally when I was young, and then, after I grew up, the dream came true -- sort of.

What happened was that when I was twenty-four years old I got poliomyelitis, or what they used to call infantile paralysis. Well, for me there wasn't anything infantile about it. I was laid up for several months, and when I finally got out of the hospital it was with the aid of a pair of crutches and later a cane. After that I did get better, but running for me was never an option. I could still dream about it, but the best I could perform was an energetic-looking shuffle. Later on I even learned to play a little tennis, but was careful never to tell my opponents that I couldn't run so they wouldn't know how easily I could be beaten if they merely hit the ball from one corner to the other.

Then one sunny day in springtime, many years later, I went back to my home town for the sixtieth reunion of my high-school graduating class. I was seventy-seven then; all of us were over seventy-five at least. Usually you only have to be sixty or sixty-five to be considered a senior, or even fifty-five in some places, so we called ourselves the Super Seniors. Our real nickname though was The Beavers.

Unbeknownst to me, the reunion organizers had planned a baseball game between us Super Seniors and a similar team from the Johnson High School Wildcats, our traditional rivals, who were, not surprisingly, also having their own sixtieth reunion celebration at the same time. Both schools were pretty small: our class had only about fifty back then when we graduated. And of course many of our classmates were unable to attend the reunion now because they were in nursing homes or had already died or had some other excuse. So that Saturday afternoon it was all we could do to put together nine old men to make up our team. I was prepared to watch with amusement from the sidelines. However, to the dismay of all concerned, we were only able to field eight players.

The others came to me and said, "Dan, why aren't you playing too? We need you."

Now, I had never actually told anybody I couldn't run. My family and some of my friends knew, of course, but never talked about it much, probably for fear of embarrassing me, and I never felt any particular need to talk about it either. It was like our own little "don't ask, don't tell" policy. If people didn't know, what they couldn't see wouldn't hurt them. I was always quite happy to let people, especially the girls, think I was perfectly normal, if they could. At least as far as walking and running were concerned. But now it had to come out. In the open. No more pretending or hiding.

"I can't run," I said.

"What do you mean, you can't run?"

"I mean I can't run. It's as simple as that."

"None of us can run much; we are all just as old as you are."

"It's not that I can't run much; it's that I can't run period. I can't get two feet off the ground at the same time, which is the Olympic definition of running. As opposed to walking."

"Well, we've gotta have you. If we can't come up with nine players we forfeit the game to the damn Wildcats. Do you want the Beavers to put their tails between their legs and go and forfeit the game?"

"No, of course not. But... "

"Well, be a sport and get on out onto the field. You can play first base where you don't have to run much. The Wildcats are just as old as we are. Just do what you can."

"But what happens when I have to bat? You can't run to first base if you can't run at all."

"Sure you can. You stand up there at the plate and maybe you get to walk on four balls, or maybe you get hit by a pitch and get to go to first base at your own leisurely pace."

"Yeah," I said, "but even if I get to first base what do I do then? If the guy next up behind me gets a hit, he might get to second base before me, and then we would both be out wouldn't we? Or just me? Or is he the one who would be out? No, I don't think it would work."

"You worry too much. Their pitcher might walk the next three batters, and you could score without having to do anything. Or the batter behind you might hit a homer, and you could score strolling in with your hands in your pockets."

"I think you are being overly optimistic."

"You have to look at it positively. You know, at the brighter side of things. Come on, let's go."

We were the "visiting" team, so we were up to bat first. And would you believe, they had me lead off. Hoping, I suppose, for a lead-off walk. It happens sometimes. My own idea was that it would be more honorable to go down swinging than to disgrace myself on the baselines, so I took a mighty cut at the very first pitch of the game, intending to strike out as soon as possible but trying to look good in the process.

As luck would have it, I connected solidly and sent a scorching roller that went right up the middle and got almost half way to the pitcher's mound. I started hobbling off toward first base, pulling my feet up one by one out of the dream-like sticky mud, knowing that I would be promptly thrown out. In fact, anybody would have been thrown out after an easy ground ball like that. Looking on ahead at the first baseman, I kept expecting to see and hear the ball smack into his mitt, ending my agony so I could head on off to the dugout. But no... he just stood there with his foot on the bag and his empty glove in the air, with a look of dismay sweeping over his countenance.

"Run, run!" I heard people shouting. So I kept on slogging away at my top speed of 3 MPH, and when I finally got to the base all safe and sound I turned around to see what had happened to the ball and what possibly could have been going on behind me.

There was some confusion and apparently arguing going on in front of the pitcher's mound, but strangely enough no one from our team seemed to be involved. As my friend Freddy described it to me later, both the pitcher and the catcher had run to pick up the ball I had hit, each one eager to become famous by scoring the first out of the game. It seems they reached the ball at the same time and both of them got their hands on it, but neither felt he could shirk his personal responsibility for supporting his team and making the play. So that's what the discussion was about as I stood there on the bag looking back. And they still had the ball.

Now what? Another infield hit will be embarrassing for me; any hit, in fact, unless it clears the fence. How am I going to get to second base? Me, a guy who can't run? It will take me a while, I thought. Maybe I'd better start now. Yes, that's what I'll do.

The pitcher had gone back up on the mound, and was examining the ball that he had finally retrieved from the catcher, apparently counting the stitches in each seam. So, while he was doing that I put my hands in my pockets and started walking down toward second base as though I were going to ask their shortstop to lend me a wad of chewing tobacco or teach me how to spit.

You may have noticed in life that it is sudden movements that attract attention. If you pass by a rattlesnake or an angry dog, the best thing to do is just act nonchalant and pay them no attention. I learned that from my Boy-Scout manual. So, I acted nonchalant, as though I knew that what I was doing was perfectly okay, and by the time the pitcher had figured out where to put his fingers on the seams and started his stretch, I was standing on the bag at second, with my hands still in my pockets, as though I had been there all morning. The pitcher looked over to first to check the runner before making his delivery. Alas, too late: no runner there. No walker either, for that matter.

That pitcher wasn't too happy when he realized I had fooled him and taken second behind his back, so to speak. In fact, he was madder than hell. So mad that he walked the next batter on four straight balls. Heck, I thought. All my clever base-stealing for nothing.

But now my fears returned; once again I had to hope against my own team; no hits, please, unless it is a homerun. Oh, I thought, if only we had a pinch runner, like the big leagues have! Well, we don't. And those Wildcats weren't going to let me walk to third this time, that's for sure. Or were they?

Their pitcher still had not cooled off from his double blows of the ball-struggle with the catcher and my walking steal from first to second. You could see he was still mad just by looking at the back of his head. Anyway, this time he got the count to one and two, and wasn't going to give the batter anything good at that point. So he gave him a high fastball inside, but a little more inside that he intended. The batter turned away, but the ball caught him behind the left shoulder in a glancing blow.

Bases loaded. Now I'm on third with no outs. This is going to be most embarrassing. Horror of horrors, I'm in a position to score the first run, and I know I can't do it. In case you forgot, because of an old affliction, I CAN'T RUN. How I got this far was only by a series of freakish miracles. My best accomplishment of the day was doubtless my quiet steal of second base, and I thought how nice life would be if only I could have died there of a heart attack or something, and gone down in history as a devoted and outstanding member of my class's sixtieth reunion baseball team. But no, I had to live on, doubtlessly destined to face the impending disgrace that was to be my fate.

At least, thought I, as long as I am alive I should try to make life as miserable as possible for my nemesis, the opposing pitcher. When he took his stretch and looked over to me at third before his delivery, I could tell by his eyebrows that he still didn't like me very much. Then I did a silly thing. I stuck my hands in my pockets and stuck my tongue out at him, and turned to face home plate as though I were going to take another sixty-foot walk. Although I was only eighteen inches off the bag, a distance that even I could handle in an emergency, he whirled and made as if to fire to the third-baseman.

Oh oh.

But he had already started his motion toward the plate before I distracted him.

BALK!

I walked on home, but in order to show respect to the opposing team and to high-five my teammates, I took my hands out of my pockets.

I had scored the winning run. It's the only time I have ever won anything in my life. And now, when I dream about running through a sticky marsh, I don't dream just about TRYING to run, but dream about SCORING runs.

THE END

The Secret

We have all heard stories about triangular love affairs in the family, like the case of a woman who falls in love with her brother-in-law, or her cousin's husband. That sort of thing. But the man who had been my sister's husband wasn't just my brother-in-law. He was my husband. And he was even more than that, as I found out one unforgettable day not long ago.

My life story would have given Edgar Allen Poe the creeps. The big blow came with a letter I found last summer in a trunk among some old clothes in the attic.

When I read that letter, every ounce of strength left my body. I must have slumped down in a dead faint, for the next thing I knew I was lying on the floor, breathing in shallow quick gasps as though I were trying to recover from a heart attack. I still had the letter in my hand, half crumpled. I looked at it again. The words were still there, the most appalling bit of information a person could possibly come upon. How could this be true, and how could I, a 48-year-old married woman, have fainted like a teen-aged girl in a Barbara Cartland novel? Let me try to explain:

In the first place, my husband is everything to me. The 27 years I have spent married to him have been a lifetime of joy and happiness. Although he is 18 years older than I, the difference in our ages has never been a problem and rarely a consideration. We have always connected on every level, and age was something we never thought about. We share our ideas and views about everything -- religion, politics, world affairs, home furnishings, family activities -- everything.

I never tire of reminiscing and looking back over the beautiful life we have had together, even though this letter I now had in my hand was appalling enough to shake a sober person's mind to the verge of insanity.

Let me give you some background. To start with, I had a happy, relatively inconsequential childhood, growing up with an older sister and two parents that saw to our upbringing with love and care. Dad was an architect and musician, and Mom was a novelist and successful homemaker, so we had plenty of erudition and culture in our family.

My parents were older than the parents of most of my classmates at school, although it never bothered me or concerned me. Dad must have been in his fifties when I was born, and Mom in her early forties at least. My sister Louise was fifteen years older than I, and that was all right too, even if it did mean I must have come along as an afterthought. They were all very active, and we had a rich family life.

The first jolt came when Louise got married. She had been living at home with us right through her college years, and then got married as soon as she graduated, when I was only eight years old. She had always been very close to me and she was a big part of my life in spite of the age difference, so I didn't know what to expect when she got married, and I was afraid I would miss her dearly when she first moved out to live with her new husband, James. I say "new" only because she was newly married to him.

James was a cousin of ours, but that didn't seem to bother anyone. I had known him from about as far back as I could remember. Even before they were married he often used to come over to our house to see Louise, and would spend many pleasant hours with me as well. When I was in kindergarten we played card games like Old Maid, and War, and he even used to play jacks and hop scotch with me. Sometimes he would swing me by the arms up over his head or carry me around the backyard on his shoulders. I delighted in his visits; it was fortunate that he lived in the same town. He was almost like a member of our happy family.

After the wedding and the honeymoon, and they were settled in at James's place, it wasn't as bad as I had feared it was going to be -- I mean the idea of losing Louise and not being able to see her much anymore. As it turned out, I was able to continue seeing them almost as much as ever. As the months went by, I probably spent as much time at their place as I did at our house. Louise arranged for my music lessons and James helped me with my homework occasionally -- things like that. I felt almost as close to James as to Louise, maybe more so.

Of course James and Louise would often visit us at our home as well. Sometimes they would read to all of us, gathered around on the sofa after dinner. But of course I knew that when James read he was really reading to me. They both liked Charles Dickens and Daphne du Maurier, so of course I did too. With Mom and Dad, the five of us also shared many other things together -- picnics, games, vacation trips to the beach, and sledding in the winter, as well as the quiet evenings at home by the fire. Those were happy years, close to James and with my other loved ones surrounding me.

As I got older, I continued to live at home, and, like Louise had done, I went through high school and college in the same city so I could stay close to my family. I saw no need to go to a university out of state as many others my age were doing.

I guess I was a junior in college when I first noticed that a change had come over my dear Louise. It was not something I could put my finger on, but she did not seem to have her accustomed vim and vigor as of old. She had lost some weight and her face was pale and already showing wrinkles more appropriate for a much older person. Although she was only 34 years old by then, she no longer felt up to walking long distances in the woods or climbing the hills behind the house where she had so often hiked with me when I was growing up. At first I attributed it to her developing maturity, thought little more about it, and continued to see her as well as James at our family dinners, birthday parties, occasional sports events and such things.

I did not do much "dating" in those years and never got very involved in school activities beyond what was necessary. I loved to read and I enjoyed long walks in the woods whether alone or with someone. I guess my family sufficed for my social life, for I was quite content the way things were. James was always just as kind to me as Louise was, almost as though he were an original member of our family. Of course, he was, in a way, being a second cousin on Mother's side, but to me he was always much more than that -- more than just a cousin or brother-in-law. He was more like the brother I never had, even though he was even older than Louise, by three or four years.

After my graduation from college I had to prove my mettle somehow, so I went into the Peace Corps for two years. However, for me, merely being apart from my loved ones was harder than facing the severe living conditions and rigorous work in the middle of Africa, so I was glad to be able to return home after I had served my time. By then Mom and Dad were getting on in years and were making plans to move into a smaller place in a retirement community where there was an assisted-living facility on the premises, available if needed.

Back in the city, I took an apartment and got a job as personnel manager for a charitable organization. I had missed my family during those years away, and focused on seeing them as much as I could. And a good thing it was, too. Dad died the day after his 80th birthday, and Mom died just a few months later. Heart broken, perhaps. In the old New England cemeteries you can see where husband and wife often died within a few days or weeks of each other. It was as though many loving couples must have felt there was not much reason to go on living, alone, without the loved one. Anyway, after Mom died I moved back into the house that held so many happy childhood memories for me.

The loss of Mom and Dad also took its toll on Louise, whose health was continuing to deteriorate. James was beautiful with her, caring and doing everything for her. I guess I had always loved James, even as a child, but loved him still more for his care of my dear sister Louise.

It turned out that Louise had a degenerative disease with no known cure, related to lymphoma. The doctors at that point gave her only a year to live. Now, strange as it may seem, in a way, that year was one of the happiest and most rewarding times of my life. James and I made a team, and the three of us were brought closer together than ever, James and I especially, in our cooperative efforts to give as much comfort and solace as possible to our precious Louise.

That was when I began to realize that my closeness and attachment to James were more than just well-developed feelings between in-laws or cousins. I loved him almost as much as I loved Louise. Maybe even more.

Louise died just as the doctors had predicted, almost to the day. James was mechanically correct during the funeral and the days immediately following, almost an automaton, but then seemed to drop into a mental vacuum of deep despair. He had loved her so. I was worried about his health and his well-being and even his sanity, as his morose state continued to worsen.

I would go over to his house and make meals for him, as I had done when Louise was with us, and as though Louise were still there. Sometimes James would set the table for us -- with three places.

He then got nervous and acted as though he did not want to see me anymore. The harder I tried to comfort him, the more he seemed to shun me and make be feel unwanted. I would be in the kitchen and I would feel his eyes on the back on my head. He would be in the doorway, but as soon as I looked around he would drop his eyes and turn his back on me, without a word. James, who had always been so warm and loving and open and communicative with me. What had I done? I wracked my brains but found no answer.

That went on for days and even weeks. For the life of me I couldn't discover what I had done to upset him so. I tried to convince him that I loved him just as much as I had loved Louise, and that I wanted to be with him just as much as ever. The more I tried, the colder he was toward me; the closer I came to him, the more he backed off or pushed me away.

Finally I got him to let it out: One evening, when I was over there making supper for him, he opened up by simply saying, "I love you. I love you too much, my dear Annabelle. My love for you has plagued me for years. I had to hide it. Hide it from Louise when she was there dying, hide it from the world, hide it from myself."

"But you couldn't hide it from me," I responded. "I have always known that, dear James. But why on earth would you WANT to hide it from me or anyone?"

"Because... " He paused. "Because I thought you would never want to marry me, your own brother-in-law."

"I think that's ridiculous. Of course I would marry you were you to ask me. Are you asking me?"

"Yes, yes, my Darling. If you don't mind what people might think."

"Who cares what people think!"

"Oh, my Love, that's exactly the way I feel. I am so glad you feel that way too," he said. "It is only in our modern society that such taboos exist, if taboo is the word. Look at history: when their wives died, the medieval kings always married their sisters-in-law if they could. In some cultures you had to, if one was available."

"Then it wouldn't be incest or anything like that... is that what you are saying?"

"Incest is just a word, Annabelle. It means nothing, my Dear. Men have married their relatives many times through the course of history."

My heart was so filled with joy at this happy moment in my life that I could hardly speak, so I let him talk on...

"The great taboo on marriage between blood relatives came with the Hapsburg royal family in Austria in the nineteenth century. Marriage between close relatives increased the likelihood of a recessive genetic disease like hemophilia, the bleeding disease. However, marriages between relatives were often arranged as a way to keep property or titles in the family. This practice got so common the Catholic Church tried to ban marriage between

106

blood relatives. And as for incest, that's another figment of modern times. When the world population was small, you had to marry a relative. That's all there was."

I was in a state of semi-dreamy happiness, listening to his beautiful soft voice run on, although it did seem to me that he was defending incest more thoroughly than necessary. He had already convinced me that it was not a consideration we need worry about. But he continued:

"In ancient Egypt a Pharaoh would often marry his sister, usually because there were no other princesses of suitably royal blood readily available. Cleopatra's father and mother were brother and sister. In fact, so were her grandfather and grandmother, and thus on back for seven generations of brother-sister marriages, or so history tells us. Incest is a product of the modern imagination, like a fad. Horses and other animals have been bred for special qualities by selective inbreeding, and they are doing fine: it's a means of improving the race."

By now I was losing interest in all this talk about incest and marriages between relatives and inbreeding. I don't know why James had to go on so about it; by then it seemed like overkill, but still it was the happiest moment in my life, now knowing that he would be my husband.

The last mental hurdle that James apparently wanted to clear up was our ages, as he said, "But, I am older than you."

"So what? You have always been older than I, although I think maybe I am catching up, at least in percentage terms," I said with a chuckle, trying to bring in a little humor. "Anyway, what difference does that make?"

I took him in my arms, and the smile returned to his face as his hands clasped my shoulders sending currents of joy throughout my body and my soul.

"Oh, James," I said, "we must be together forever."

"Yes, forever," he replied.

We waited a suitable period of time out of respect for dear Louise (and for what people might think, as it were) a slow but agonizing period of anticipation for me. Finally we were married in a little chapel in the hills where the family -- all five or us -- used to spend holiday weekends so many years ago.

And we have been very happy together ever since: twenty-seven years it has been.

Then a couple of months ago I was cleaning out a trunk that still had some of Louise's things in it that should have been given to the Salvation Army or the Goodwill people, and I found an old letter that Mother had written to her.

I opened it, looked at it, and suddenly it was as though I were hit by a sledgehammer. I was immediately sick to my stomach and thought I might throw up, but didn't. That wouldn't have done any good. So I fainted instead, overwhelmed and astounded by what I had read.

Lying there, I gradually tried to pull myself together; I had to wipe my chin off with the hem of my skirt as I dragged myself up from the floor on to an easy chair, trying to recover from this shocking nightmare. I still had the letter, squeezing it in my hand. I looked at it again, on the second page, where it read, in part:

"... Louise, my dear, please know that your father and I still love you nevertheless. We will adopt the baby; she will be ours and will be your younger sister. You will go on with your studies and finish high school and then you will go on to college and complete your education. I will not have you living the horrible life of a single mother, and the young man is in no position to take on a 15-year-old bride. When you complete your education and come of age you may marry whomever you choose, be it this one if he can wait that long, or another young man who is worthy of you. It goes without saying that your father and I are not happy with your behavior, but familial love must be dearer than social propriety. Please know that we still love you, and always will. And we will love and care for your precious little Annabelle, who will be our dear daughter as well as our granddaughter. My heart is filled with both sadness and joy. -- Mum."

As I slowly came to, I had to read the letter two or three times before its significance really sank in.

Louise, my sister, was my mother? My mother was my grandmother? Is that why she was older than the mothers of my school friends?

Oh, dear Lord, what will James think when he learns he married Louise's daughter and not her sister? And finds out that he's not my brother-in-law but my step-father! My husband is my step-father!

And... oh...! Oh no, it can't be true.! But what if... Oh my God! James...! Is that why Mom was always a little cold toward James? Or had I imagined it? The wildest conceivable ideas raced through my stricken mind. I must find out when he met Louise -- how old they were. Could he be...? The thought was madness... impossible!

I fell back down into the chair again, with the world reeling around me, with a splitting headache, wishing I could faint once more and wake up to learn it was all a bad dream. A nightmare. I began to recall the things James had said about incest the day he proposed to me, how incest was so insignificant as to be unworthy of consideration. He made quite a point of it then, as I recall, stressing how unimportant it was. Could he know something more, that he has never told me? Yes, he must know... No, that's impossible -- we have always shared all our most intimate thoughts and feelings. He has never held anything back from me. It must be that he doesn't know. Or maybe it's not true, not so frightful as my imagination has made it. No, it can't be true. Or if it is, James can't possibly have known. No way.

But now I have this letter and I must tell him. I must find out for sure. I will have to tell him some day anyway. Oh dear, how can I go on with this?

I couldn't sleep that night in my distraught state. James would realize something was wrong.

The next morning when he looked at me, he knew something frightful had happened. He could see I was sick and wanted to take me to the hospital. My pulse was fast and pitifully weak. I was feverish, short of breath, wild eyed. I could not have been a pretty sight.

"What is it? Tell me what happened, my darling."

"I found a letter written a long time ago."

"A letter?"

"From my mother to my sister Louise, before I was born."

"Darling, you look terribly upset. You mustn't let yourself get so upset just by a letter."

Now, I have always believed it was important to have your reason dominate your emotions, and if there was ever a time for reason, it was now.

"James," I said as I sat down, trying to maintain my composure, "we have to have a talk. I have to talk to you."

"Yes, I know," he calmly replied with his quiet voice and the gentle, understanding manner that I had always known and loved.

"You know what I want to talk about?"

"Maybe. I'm not sure. Tell me, my Darling."

THE ORIGINAL END

111

Author's note

Some of my friends said they were left unsatisfied and frustrated with this ending (which of course smacks of the endings of "The French Lieutenant's Woman" or "The Lady or the Tiger"), and persuaded me to write an epilogue. As I saw it, the epilogue could have taken either one of two directions. In one of them the distraught young woman would have been overcome by fears of what Society might think, and would have promptly committed suicide or moved into a nunnery for the rest of her life. This is the other possibility:

Epilogue

"The letter," he said, "do you want to read it to me?"

"I... I can't... Here, you read it."

I gave him the letter and he read it in silence. I don't know what I expected from him -- some violent reaction, I guess. But no, his face was impassive and his voice silent, as he re-read the letter. Then he came and took me in his arms.

My darling Annabelle, you mean so much to me. I have loved you ever since we played hop-scotch and Old Maid together when you were a child. There is nothing -- nothing in the world -- that could ever make me change the way I feel about you.

"But... but... " I stammered.

112

"But let's not forget that you are all that I care about. We have each other. You are my life and my love, and that's all that matters."

As if this were not enough, the overwhelming possibility was still pounding in my mind as I looked into his kindly, loving eyes. I had to find out.

"When did you first know Louise?" I asked.

"Almost all my life," he answered.

"No. I mean when did you first really know her? How old were you? How old was she?"

"I am sure we saw each other when we were tiny children, but I especially remember seeing her again when I was a senior in high school and she was a freshman. I was 17 and she was 14. That was when I first realized I was in love with her."

The ominous significance of these words, and their possible implications, threatened to throw me into another faint.

In a flash, I even thought, oh, if only I could just die... But that would solve nothing. The facts would still be there. My head was pounding and threatening to explode. "Then maybe you're... " I stammered.

James's soothing voice kept on: "You are everything to me Annabelle. Yes, I'm your father too. I loved you before

113

you were born, and it was my lifetime grief that I could not do more for you from the start. You are everything in the world to me."

I tried to think with my head pounding and my brain in turmoil once again. "So... " the words stuck in my throat. "So... you are my cousin, and my brother-in-law, and my husband of 27 years, and now my father too." I had to put my arms around him to keep from collapsing again. As my overwhelming emotions swept through my body, I grasped him ever more tightly. And in that one short moment I realized that nothing in any old letter could affect my love for him.

"My Darling," he repeated, "those are just words. You are my life and my love and my all. And that's everything that matters."

Oh, what to do? I was choked up with emotion and wild thoughts were still flashing across my mind. Shall I crawl off and die? What good would that do? It wouldn't change the facts. Can it be, I wondered, that incest doesn't really mean anything, like he says? Can I go on living with him? Could I ever go on living WITHOUT him? Without him and his love in my life? No, of course I couldn't. He was too much a part of my life. He WAS my life. This man here in my arms, my cousin, brother-in-law, my husband, and my father, and my everything. Who else in the world was ever able to have all those dear people so close together, all at once, rolled into one? I began to realize how lucky and blessed I was.

I could only cling to him and answer my own question, "Yes, and you are everything to me too," I heard myself whispering into his ear. I took a deep breath, feeling relieved that I had been able to lift the weight of secretly bearing something that I had believed he did not know. My tension relaxed, my headache miraculously disappeared, and I realized then that my love for him was greater than anything else in the world, greater than any letter, greater than any old taboos, greater than what anybody might think.

"But," I added, now breathing easily again, "let's keep it a secret, shall we?"

"Yes. We'll keep it a secret. We wouldn't want people to talk."

THE FINAL END

Author's note

In this story I did not discuss the question of James and Annabelle's having children. I thought that might complicate matters.

I Didn't Know

Have you ever noticed that among some living things there are parts that seem to be faster to develop than other parts, and other parts that are slower to develop, so that things seem to be, like, out of balance? Like a young colt has legs that are too long, or a Labrador puppy has feet that are too big. While babies have feet and legs that are way too small.

And sometimes teenagers have parts that don't all develop at the same rate. Take my youngest sister, Trudy, for instance. (Her real name is Gertrude, but you can see why she likes to be called Trudy. "Gertrude" is almost as bad as "Ludmilda" or "Goneril" or some other Scandinavian witch.)

Anyway, Trudy's development has been manifestly uneven. There is a definite break right around the Adam's apple, or where her Adam's apple would be if she had an Adam's apple. Trudy is fourteen, and her development above the neck has not kept up with her development below. Oh, she isn't really dumb -- not all the time -- but occasionally her stupidity takes on enormous proportions. Like when she and her cousin Sally went to the movies the other day.

We live in a suburb about fifteen miles out from the Big City, but we are near the station and it's easy to take the

117

commuter train in. Although they call them commuters, the trains run every half hour all day long. Here in the suburbs we get regular movies at the local Plaza Theater with its eight screens, but we never get foreign films or the exotic art films that have won prizes at the Cannes Film Festival or anything like that. So last Saturday, Trudy and Sally decided they just had to go into the City to see this *outré* French film they had heard about. Now maybe my family is a little more conservative than most, but my other sister, Elizabeth, who is nineteen, and I, who am twenty, were never allowed to go into the City alone until we were sixteen years old. But Trudy and her cousin harangued and harangued until Mom said okay. (Dad was away on a business trip to London.) Mom figured that since it was a matinée and they would be home for dinner it would be okay.

Before she left I specifically told Trudy to watch out for her money, for there are plenty of thieves and pick-pockets lurking about these days. She was wearing a yellow blouse and fitted slacks, and had her coin purse in her hip pocket, making a clear outline and an inviting target. "You can't go like that," I said. "You'll have to find some other place for your purse."

"But where?" she answered. "I'm not going to hold it in my hand all day, and I don't want to have to carry a handbag just for that."

"Put it in your brassière," I said, "in the middle. You have plenty of room."

"Har har. Very funny... Well, okay."

118

So that's what she did. And off they went.

-        -   -

Trudy got back home around seven-thirty, just about suppertime, terribly upset, with cheeks flushed, throat choked up, and tears in her eyes. I was there when she came in. "What on earth happened?" I asked. "Didn't you go to the movie?"

"Yes, we went to the movie," she babbled.

"Well, something happened, that's clear. What was it?"

"I've been robbed."

"Robbed?" I replied in astonishment. "But we talked about how you have to be careful that way. How did you manage to be robbed?"

Still sobbing, Trudy started in: "When we got there, the movie hadn't begun yet and the lights were still on, but the place was almost full. There were a few empty seats at the back, so Sally and I went on in and sat down."

"All right," I said, "and then what?"

"Well, a minute or two later this boy came into our row and very politely asked, 'Is this seat taken?' and sat down next to me before I could say anything. I wouldn't have known what to say anyway. He wasn't bad looking and seemed quite nice in fact. He said his name was Al. Then the movie began and he didn't say anything else."

119

"So?"

"When the movie was about half over he got up and left. I thought he was going to the men's room. But he didn't come back. Then a few minutes later I realized he had taken my purse."

"What! You mean he was able to slip his hand inside there and get your money without you feeling anything?"

"I didn't know that that was what he was trying to do."

Like I said, Trudy's mental development has not kept up with the rest of her.

THE END

College Tuition

You know, in this country, we still live in a male-oriented or male-dominated or male-preferential society, or whatever you want to call it. So, we women either can try to be activists like Susan B. Anthony and Gloria Steinam, or else we can accept the hand we have been dealt and try to make the best of it. I figured that since most activists take one or two generations to make a significant impact, I would choose the latter course and make the best of the situation as it was.

I'll tell you what I mean:

To begin with, my parents were both pretty old fashioned. They lived on a farm in Upstate New York and had never been to college or anything like that. By the time my brother Chip and I were in high school, Dad was already getting old and thinking of retiring. Small family farms weren't doing too well by then anyway, because of the competition of the big corporate farming concerns, and the small piece of land we owned was soon worth more for development of suburban sprawl than for farming. Chip, who was two years older than I, was the first one in the family ever to go to college, and after Dad sold off most of the land there was just enough money to pay for both Chip's college education and a modest annuity that was sufficient to support Mom and Dad for the rest of their years. I had hoped to go to college too, but Dad saw no need for a woman to waste that money on education. He was still of the old school that a woman's place is in the home, barefoot with the children or whatever.

In high school I always had good grades and was active in athletics and other extracurricular activities; I was even vice president of my class junior year. So right at the beginning of my senior year I started sending out applications for scholarships along with the applications for admission to ten or a dozen different colleges. I wanted to study English Literature and Creative Writing, but most of the scholarships they were offering seemed to focus either on budding scientists and engineers, or on descendants of Mayflower Pilgrims and First Families of Virginia. The only scholarship I was offered was one thousand dollars given in memory of Emily Dickinson. But the tuition was eleven thousand dollars and room and board almost eight thousand, so one thousand wouldn't go far. I could have planned to take a part-time job as a waitress or dishwasher at minimum wage, but that never would have been enough to make up the difference. And besides, I really wanted to devote myself to my studies, try for Phi Beta Kappa if I could, and prove to my family and myself that college wasn't just for boys.

So I had to think of something else, and I'll tell you what I came up with: without telling my parents or even my brother, Chip, I went over to the next county and took out my own post-office box. Then I went home, got on my typewriter and wrote up an ad for the "personals" column in the city newspaper. It read as follows:

SWF Single white female VIRGIN, tall, slim, nineteen years old, needs money for college tuition. Willing to auction self off for one-night stand to highest bidder. (Men only, please.) Submit sealed bids and photograph before August 15 to Desirée at PO Box 269, Whitewater Falls, NY 12899.

I figured I had one possession that was valuable -- my virginity -- and that I might as well take advantage of it. While I still had it. I mean, a college education was the most important thing in the world to me, and that's what I wanted, at all costs.

I waited until August 18 before I went back to the PO Box to see what answers I had collected and pick them up all at once. To my surprise there were 67 responses. They covered a wide range of bids from an insulting low of $50 to a crazy high of -- believe it or not -- $25,001. I was glad I had had the foresight to ask for the photograph, although not every response included a picture. A few of the photos that I did get looked rather horrible -- definitely not suitable. I picked one who was not too bad looking who had offered $18,000 and decided I would go for it.

And it worked out fine. We met in a hotel downtown and exchanged the precious goods as we had planned. He was obviously a millionaire and seemed quite satisfied with the arrangement. And it was just enough money for me to go through my freshman year reasonably comfortably. Of course I never let my parents know where my financial good luck had come from; I cooked up a story about having won a fat scholarship from the Society for the Preservation of the Memory of Dead Poets of America, and they never bothered to question it.

I went through freshman year in good style; I got mostly A's and a few B's. I enjoyed my courses and new friends as well as other school activities. My only disappointment was the indifferent attitude that Mom, and especially Dad, continued to maintain regarding my education. I could never convince him that college was a woman's place as much as a man's place, so when the time came to plan for the next fall term, I was more determined than ever to make a name for myself in the world of books and erudition. I would get straight A's or die trying.

There was only one problem, which was the same problem I had met so cleverly the year before, the problem of money. And now I had to think of some way to finance my sophomore year. Finally in late July I got an idea and had my inspiration. I went to my typewriter and began typing:

SWF Single white female VIRGIN, tall, slim, twenty years old, needs money for college tuition ...

THE END

The Grudge

I think I will become a nun, or maybe a Lesbian. No boys for me. They are horrible.

And boys can harbor a grudge too. Wow, can they ever! I can't stand boys; I never want to see one again.

I wasn't always this way -- I mean, my attitude toward boys. In grade school I was just like the other girls, curious about boys perhaps, but ignorant as anything. Then when I was about eight years old I got hold of a couple of old medical books of my father's that I found in a box in the basement, and read a clinical description of how women got pregnant and how babies were born. I thought it all sounded pretty disgusting, and it was five or six years later before my interest in the matter resurfaced.

Yes, when we were about fourteen we did start playing around with boys a little, but I remembered enough from the old medical book to concentrate on protecting the area below the belt, from hips to my thighs. However, I admit that when I was that age the boys did start to seem exciting, although I would never have told them so. I knew enough to know that I didn't want to get pregnant by having too much fun or investigating too much.

Then there was this girl Deirdre in our neighborhood who acted as though she knew so much -- about boys that is. And it's true, she did know quite a lot. We used to compare notes and ideas and "how far we had gone," or how much "necking" or "petting" we had done with one boy or another. She was the one who first explained how you could have almost as much fun and thrill by doing some other things than the real business. Of course, I certainly wasn't about to enter into anything like the real thing, at my tender age and with my overwhelming fear of pregnancy.

Deirdre started talking about "oral sex." I knew that "oral" meant the mouth, and to me that meant kissing, which couldn't have been too naughty or sinful as I saw it. People in my family were always kissing each other, although I admit that kissing a boy was several notches better than being slobbered on by my Great Aunt Priscilla. Ricky was the boy that I liked best to kiss. Six or eight of us used to go over to his house where he had a pool table and a couple of couches in the basement and play games: pool, and darts, and things like that, and one that was particularly popular called "photography," where you turn out the lights and see what develops. Ha ha.

Now I have to tell you something sad about me and Ricky. We are both pretty smart, and maybe that's what interested us in each other in the first place. However, something came between us at school one day last month. We had a spelling bee, and Ricky and I were the last two standing after all the others had been eliminated. We both got three more words right, and then, as you have probably guessed by now, Ricky missed one. He misspelled "benefitted" insisting it should have two "t's," like "fitted." So I won.

Ricky's face went ashen white, and then flushed crimson, but only for a moment. He quickly recovered his normal, relaxed countenance, smiled sweetly and gently said, "That's okay, I'll get you next time." I thought no more about it. I would have hated the idea of his bearing a grudge because I had won out over him; some men cannot bear the thought of being beaten by a woman in anything. Fortunately Ricky wasn't that way. After that he continued to be just as friendly as ever toward me, and even kissed me a couple more times at the photography games and things like that. Those evenings were always a lot of fun, there with Ricky and my other friends, especially the kissing, which was especially nice and always seemed to make you want a little more.

So one dark evening last summer when the clouds were low and there wasn't any moon, Ricky and I slipped out and got in his parents' car which was parked in the driveway. He had heard about oral sex from Deirdre, he said, so I started to kiss him, very politely at first, then a little more vigorously, and then I began poking around a little with my tongue. I like this oral sex, I thought. I was surprised at how much fun it was, especially when he poked back and began to caress my neck and shoulder at the same time. Then he asked, "Do you like oral sex?"

Well, this tasted pretty good to me, so I modestly replied, "Yes, I think it's rather nice." That's when he pulled up my dress and pushed his head between my knees and started kissing me DOWN THERE. Suddenly it dawned on me that oral sex wasn't just oral. But after I had said it was nice I couldn't let on how ignorant I was and admit I didn't know what I was talking about. So I didn't say anything more and let him go on playing around down there to see what would happen. He kept on for a little while longer, and I must admit it was even more than nice; it was delightful, superb, glorious. I was in some sort of seventh heaven, discovering a joy that far exceeded the pleasures of my wildest dreams or fantastic imaginations. I didn't know whether to tell him to stop, or not to stop, so I told him not to stop.

But after about half an hour he stopped anyway, and by then I was ready for a little rest. But he took my hand and put it between his legs and said, "Would you like to try it?" I had to think a minute before I realized what he was driving at. He wanted me to do the same thing to him that he had done to me, sort of. I was still remembering what I had said about oral sex being nice, and didn't want to appear too stupid, so I let him guide my attention down to where his excitement was concentrated. I found his equipment right there where it was supposed to be, and with a little encouragement and slight pressure from his left hand on the back of my neck, I, well, gave him the pleasure he was craving, and was surprised at how much pleasure it gave me at the same time. Made me feel close to him, you might say. I was really beginning to like Ricky a lot. He had completely forgotten his grudge and his animosity toward me from the spelling bee.

After a little while he said, "We'd better stop; it's getting late."

"Okay," I said, "I guess you're right."

128

We got out of the car, and as there wasn't anybody else around I took him in my arms and started to give him a normal goodnight kiss. He backed away slightly, with his hands on my forearms, "You don't think I could kiss a filthy dirty mouth that had just been doing what yours has been doing, do you?"

I was stunned. I think I will become a nun or maybe a Lesbian. No boys for me. I never want to see one again. They are horrible.

THE END

Thirty of the Best Short Stories

Horses

I am not as young as I used to be; I'll admit it. So I know I don't remember names and dates and a few other things as well as I once did, but in some things I am better now than I ever was before. Like horses.

I have always loved horses: looking at them, riding them as a kid, petting them, feeding them, but especially betting on them. And I have made money on the horses from time to time, although I confess I have also lost a bit on occasion. But I have studied horses, visited a good many race tracks and stables, and reviewed the histories of dozens of horses at the track and in the record books.

I don't have a foolproof system; I'll admit that too. You might say that I have a lot of systems. I look at horses' legs, their mouths, their ears, their chests. I study the history of their trainers and owners and jockeys. I examine their pedigrees and their ancestry and the records of their equine relatives.

Often the information or clues I have developed regarding a horse have not been consistent. I mean, racehorses usually seem to have some good things and some bad things going for them. Sometimes a horse may have an owner like the Whitney's with a good record, and a good string of ancestors like War Admiral and Count Fleet, but have legs or teeth that don't look so good. I wouldn't

131

bet much in such a case. Maybe a little, but not much. Over the years I am somewhat ahead, although in some months I have barely broken even.

Almost all of the guys you talk to have made money at the track, or so they say. I sometimes wonder whether they are just saying so in order to make themselves sound important and clever, or whether there is something in a person's psyche that makes him remember the good times and forget the bad times. And if that's so, maybe it's a good thing: I guess if we could only remember the bad times we wouldn't want to bother to go on living.

Anyway, that's the way horses have always come across to me; every horse has some positive aspects and some negative aspects. You bet when you find a horse that seems to have a better-than-average positive/negative ratio.

Well, a while ago I identified a horse named BUTTER FLYER that did not fit into this mold. He was scheduled to run the following Saturday afternoon at Hialeah. I mean, I could not find anything wrong with him. No negative qualities. None whatsoever. His ancestors were consistent winners, but were mostly from Argentina and Ireland so he had not gained fame at Santa Anita or even Charles Town. And therefore the odds on him were good. He had been trained at a good stable, had a good jockey, and had those strong, wiry, long legs you love to look at.

Early odds on him were quoted at fourteen to one, probably because he had never run before at Hialeah, and, to most of the ignorant bettors, he was an unknown. The masses prefer to bet on a horse they know, or at least have heard of, regardless of how good he is, rather than bet on anything smacking of the unknown. But this BUTTER FLYER wasn't unknown to me; I had done my homework and I knew he was good.

Now, as I said before, I am not a young as I used to be, and I have been thinking of retiring and living in South Florida full time. I have some money, but I could use a little more to pay for the move and the cost of getting settled in a new place. So, as you have by now surmised, I decided to scrape together what money I could gather up, without selling my soul, and put it on BUTTER FLYER on the nose, for this time I had found a horse that couldn't lose.

The guy that ran the off-track betting operation near where I lived was a fellow named Giaccomo Cavalieri. Not surprisingly, he was known around the neighborhood as simply Jocko. I do not doubt that he was working for the Mafia, but in our town the Mafia runs most things, and they keep operations like off-track betting smooth and honest (after taking their cut, of course). I wouldn't trust Jocko with my girlfriend or the keys to my car, but he had taken many of my bets before, and as far as I know he had always dealt honestly with bets on the horses, because otherwise the Mafia would have been on his neck. They keep their illegal book-making operation clean and have never been known to renege on a bet on the horses.

I was able to gather together $1,500 dollars which I put in an envelope with a note to Jocko telling him to place my bet half an hour before the race. A big bet placed further ahead of time could significantly alter the odds, in an unfavorable direction.

Then I had to wait. I knew I would be a nervous wreck if I sat on the edge of my chair until the race results came in, so I convinced myself to be nonchalant and went to the beach for the weekend. It was a sure thing, so why should I sweat it? I even waited until Sunday morning to casually check the race results in the paper, and sure enough, just as I had predicted, BUTTER FLYER came in first in his race and paid $29.50 to win. I had made $20,625, which would come to $18,562.50 after Jocko and the Mafia took out their standard ten per cent from all winnings.

Monday evening I went back to the bar where Jocko hangs out. Although Jocko wasn't there, I was in a generous mood and bought drinks for all my friends, and some mere acquaintances, and some people I didn't even know.

"Where's Jocko tonight?" I asked the bartender.

"He was here earlier and paid off the only two guys who won anything on the horses over the weekend," he replied. "He went on home saying he wasn't feeling too well."

"Oh, he did, did he? Well, we'll see about that."

I went out to the car, got my cell phone and called Jocko. He sounded annoyed at my call. "I want my money," I said. "have you got my money?"

"What money? What are you talking about?" he answered.

"What am I talking about? I'm talking about BUTTER FLYER who won on Saturday and paid better than fourteen to one."

"Yeah, so what? What does BUTTER FLYER have to do with price of eggs?"

"What are you trying to pull? I put $1,500 on BUTTER FLYER on the nose and he paid $29.50. I want my money, and according to my calculation that's $18,562.50 after you and your Mafia friends have taken your fat cut."

"I don't know what you are talking about." And with that he hung up the phone.

I was furious, as you can imagine. What kind of a fast one was he trying to pull, anyway? Some unscrupulous bookies have been known to pocket money coming in for bets on long shots that they thought had no chance of winning, and some have made quite a lot on the side that way. So, Gioccomo Cavalieri has pocketed my $1,500 and denies that I ever placed the bet! I had always trusted Jocko before, and all our dealings, which of course were technically illegal in our town, had been verbal so as not to leave any embarrassing footprints. But I never imagined he would turn out to be a crook as well as a criminal.

I was still seeing red, and all sorts of thoughts ran through my mind, especially the idea that he might be planning to go retire in Mexico at my expense. Yes, he probably had some cowardly scheme like that in mind. Well, I had better hurry if I was going to get my money.

Fortunately I had a Colt .38 automatic in my glove compartment that I only use for emergencies. Okay, this was an emergency, and the more I thought about how much of an emergency it was, the madder I got.

When I got near Jocko's place, I parked the car in a side street, stuck the Colt into my inside coat pocket, and went straight on in. Jocko was right there in the living room, with sort of a phony sweet smile on his face mixed with some questioning wrinkles between his eyebrows. "What are you doing here?" he said, "I don't do business at home. We do business at the bar; you know that. I'll be there at nine-o-clock tomorrow evening."

"Don't give me that. What are you trying to pull, anyway? I want my dough and I want it now."

"What dough? What are you talking about?" He could see that I was really mad, and his voice began to waver.

"My dough from BUTTER FLYER, like I said on the phone."

"You're crazy," he said.

That's when I pulled out the gun and pointed it straight at him. "Well, I may be crazy but this gun is not. Let's have the money, eighteen thousand five hundred and change."

"You gotta be kidding," and he reached for the gun. Now, I hadn't really intended to kill the son-of-a-bitch; I just wanted the money that was my due. But the gun went off, and must have hit him straight in the heart, for he collapsed and died immediately. Right there on the floor in front of me.

"Oh, Hell," I thought. "Now I'm the one who will have to go to Mexico."

Guys like Jocko deserve to die; I'm only sorry that I was the man who had to do it. What I should of done was try and find one of Jocko's bosses up the line in the Mafia hierarchy, and I'll bet they would have taken care of him. But too late now. My story would never hold up. Now I had to get out of there. Out of town. Out of the country. Out of sight.

I went home to pack a razor, toothbrush, some underwear, and a couple of other essentials. I would fly to Mexico tomorrow morning. I'm not going to spend the rest of my life in prison for knocking off some scumbug like Jocko. I got what money I had left out of my bedroom safe; fortunately I had not put absolutely everything on BUTTER FLYER, although I was going to miss that fifteen hundred, not to mention the eighteen thousand that should have been mine.

However, as it turned out, when I was looking through my wallet on the plane to Mexico City the next day, I found that I had exactly fifteen hundred dollars more than I expected. I still had the letter to Giocomo Cavalieri instructing him to bet on BUTTER FLYER and had forgotten to give it to him. And the fifteen hundred dollars was there, inside, intact.

137

I had killed poor Jocko for nothing. Oh well, he was a scumbug.

THE END

I Wasn't Quite Able

All this talk we are hearing about gays in the military reminds me of an incident that happened a few years ago. To begin with, I want you to know that I don't think I am particularly prejudiced, but sometimes you have to be practical nevertheless.

For instance, right after Bill Clinton was elected in 1992, I wrote him a letter telling him that as president he was going to have a problem with gays in the military. I suggested two practical possibilities for handling the matter, although he chose a third, which you know as "Don't ask, don't tell."

But all that's another story.

This story today takes place in Key West, Florida, which is about as remote a place as you can get to in eastern USA without a boat. It's like Provincetown, Massachusetts that way. And as anyone who has visited those spots is aware, it is also like Provincetown for its reputation as a place where gays and Lesbians like to congregate. (Why do we always say "gays and Lesbians" and not "Lesbians and gays?" Is it another instance of macho discrimination against women?)

I have a cousin who lives with her husband in Key West, both very conservative and both very straight, as it were. I went to visit them a couple of years ago. Drove all the

139

way, and let me tell you, it's a long drive from anywhere. (Did you know that from Pensacola to Key West is as far as it is from Pensacola as Chicago?)

Well, my cousin and her husband live right in the town, on a short street called Love Lane. They had told me it was downtown, near the library. A short walk, they said. Park in front of the library and walk from there, were my instructions. I had a little map of Key West, and I could see where the library was, but Love Lane wasn't on the map. I did as I was told, parked my car in front of the library, got out and started walking around the library looking for Love Lane. I walked two blocks in every direction, with no luck.

This was before I had a cell phone, and I was getting tired. By then the sun had set and it was beginning to get dark. Maybe Love Lane was even too small to have a street sign and I was going right by it. I'll ask someone, I thought. But there was nobody in sight. That part of town seemed deserted. Maybe everybody from the neighborhood had gathered at the seawall to watch the sun go down, a Key West tradition I learned about later. Finally I saw two men coming toward me on the other side of the street. Maybe they know.

I started to cross over. They were both pretty big guys, three or four inches taller than I, and obviously were types that worked out or pumped iron. One had on a T shirt with cutaway shoulders displaying his well-developed and well-tattooed deltoids, and the other, who was even bigger, was wearing fitted blue jeans and a matching shirt with three buttons open at the neck. They seemed to be friends, and

140

were holding hands as they came swinging down the street with a jaunty bounce to their step.

"Excuse me, could either of you gentlemen... uh... tell me where Love Lane is?" were the words that were on my lips.

But I wasn't quite able to open my mouth and get them out.

THE END

Thirty of the Best Short Stories

It's Your Cow

I don't know for sure whether this story is actually true or not, but I do know that there are two adjoining farms about fifteen miles up the road from where we live, and that is where it all takes place, so maybe it really is true.

We live in southwestern Wisconsin, and it is definitely cow country. Nowadays most of the newer establishments are run by specialized dairy corporations, and cows are all they do. The older, more traditional, family-run farms are slowly dying out, but there are still a few of them around -- farms where they grow a little corn and enough vegetables to supply their own needs and still have some to sell off at the farmers' market on Saturday mornings. And all these little farms have some animals, especially cows, of course. We are proud of our cows, as you can plainly see if you have ever been to one of the county fairs we still have in Wisconsin almost every year.

At the fairs we have contests with judges for all sorts of animals, including chickens and turkeys, and sheep and goats, and even pigs and horses, but especially cows, which always constitute the main event. Some of the farmers around here have but one main goal in life, and that is to win the prize at the fair for the best cow in their breed or class. So they are just as careful in the selective breeding of their bovine species as are the equine breeders of the finest Kentucky race horses.

143

One of these farms is owned and run by a fellow named Oscar Adamson, and Oscar owns a bull that recently won a blue ribbon at the county fair. That blue ribbon meant a lot to Oscar, and he is most extremely proud of it. But Oscar also has some business sense, and to make the best of a good thing he has put the bull up for stud at a pretty good fee.

And this is were the story begins.

The farm adjacent to the Adamson place is owned by a friend of Oscar's, named Ezekiel McHenry, who has a couple of heifers that also did pretty well in the last competition and are ready to be bred. Oscar is a nice guy, and since his friend Ezekiel is the first to engage the services of the blue-ribbon bull, he is giving him a special rate for the stud service.

Oscar also has a sixteen-year-old daughter, Lou Ann Adamson, who is one of the cutest girls in the neighborhood. Jimmy McHenry, the youngest of the four McHenry boys, is fifteen and a half, but big for his age. He has been chasing after Lou Ann for a couple of months, but has never been able to get to first base with her. Lou Ann is a good girl and does a lot of work around the farm, always reads her Bible like her mother told her to do, and goes to church regularly. And she steadfastly resists Jimmy's amorous advances with the assertion that she is not old enough to do things like that. However Jimmy keeps trying and hoping anyway.

When the time comes for Farmer Adamson to send his bull over to the McHenry farm for the stud service, it is Lou Ann's task and responsibility to take the bull across to the paddock where the cow is waiting. Jimmy is there when she arrives and he opens the gate to let the bull in. Then the two kids get up on the fence and sit there, watching.

After a while the bull starts getting interested and begins to get to work. Jimmy, sitting next to Lou Ann, moves a little closer and holds her hand. She lets him hold her hand, but makes sure that that is all he holds, for her daddy has told her to watch out for boys, especially young farm boys who know too much. But Jimmy is getting excited looking at the bull, and can't restrain himself. He blurts out:

"Wow! I'd like to be doing that right now!"

"Well," says Lou Ann, unabashed and with a perfectly straight face, "go ahead. It's your cow."

THE END

The Double Agent

I am an American citizen although I was born in Moscow, in 1946. My father was military attaché at the US Embassy, having served with some distinction during the war as an adviser to the 47th Division of the Soviet Army fighting against the Germans. Dad liked Russia and admired the Russians and their tenacious resistance during the war, and I think his assignment to the Embassy was sort of a reward for his rather valiant service. That's where he met my mother, who was Russian and had been working for the Embassy as an interpreter, so it was easy for them to get to know each other and fall in love and get married.

I think I started speaking Russian before English, as not only my mother but also the nurse that took care of me when my parents were working was of course Russian. Almost the first thing I remember was my father telling me about the United States and how he would soon take us back to his beloved Vermont where he and his own parents had grown up.

But unfortunately that was never to be. Dad was killed in a strange accident, shot in the head while accompanying a Soviet regiment on military maneuvers in the Ural Mountains. But my mother still had her job at the Embassy, and although I was very young I had already started kindergarten. Mom said that one day she would take me to the United States but that it would have to wait a while.

I actually liked school, although in the USSR the kids always had to line up and march everywhere, into class, into the gymnasium, onto the field for sports events like soccer or track. However, the regimentation and marching around didn't bother me. And I didn't mind the rigid organization of the educational system, for it seemed to bring me and my schoolmates closer together and gave me a chance, by the time I was twelve years old, to take on a position of Youth Leader in one of the sections of the Young Communists Organization.

I never believed a lot of the talk and stuff they gave us about the glories and importance of the State, and the sacrifices that patriotic comrades should make for the good of the Nation, and all that, but I went through the motions anyway. What made it tolerable, and even sort of fun, was that my friends were there with me, doing it too. However, I was still interested in my American heritage, and Mom again promised me that sometime we would go and live in the United States, as Dad had wanted.

Finally, when I was thirteen, Mom made the break, and came to Vermont, where she had lined up a position teaching Russian at the Middlebury College Language School. It was very exciting for me, as until that time I had only heard about America but never been there.

High school in Vermont was quite different from what I had known in Russia, but I have always been studious, and I liked school in the US too, although classes were bigger and not so tightly organized as they had been before. In fact, it seemed as though there was almost no organization or discipline at all in my American high school, but I didn't mind the chaos. To me it only meant that you could do just about anything you wanted to do, quite a change from the tight routine I had known in Russia.

When the time came for me to go to college, I got a good scholarship right there because of my mother's position on the Middlebury faculty, and I breezed through with a double major in history and political science. They even had me giving talks about what life and school had been like in the Soviet Union, although it had been five or six years since I had left the USSR and come to America.

I knew I was interested in foreign affairs, and the summer after my junior year I got a pretty good deal as a summer intern at the Department of State, in DRS, the Division of Research for the Soviet Union. The money I made there was even more than I needed to see me through my senior year at college. So as I was getting ready to graduate I was already making plans to go back to the State Department again to see what they might have for me this time, maybe even on a permanent basis.

But it didn't happen. What happened was that I was asked for an interview by a representative of Another Agency that week in the spring when the recruiters come around to the colleges. He was particularly interested in the fact that I spoke Russian and knew something of Russian life and culture from my early years. In case I didn't make it clear, he was from the CIA. He went on to say how the CIA could offer me a much better starting position than the State Department could, and how with them I would be doing more immediate good for my country because the CIA was an active organization of devoted patriots and the State Department was a passive bunch of cookie pushers and tea drinkers.

I didn't know there was that much difference between the two organizations, but the immediacy of the CIA offer and the man's guarantee of active work overseas made the difference in my mind. So six weeks later I was in Langley, Virginia getting my orders to go to Camp Peary for counter-intelligence training. Ten months later I was a CIA special operative under the DDO, Deputy Director for Operations.

I was disappointed with my first two assignments, which attached me to US Embassies, first in Chile and then in Guatemala. I had hoped to go back to Russia, thinking I might be able to look up some of my old school friends that I hadn't seen in ten years. It seems "The Company," as the CIA often liked to call itself, wanted to test me a little at first, but at least they had me working on problems of Soviet infiltration into government agencies and corporate organizations in those Hispanic countries. It was the beginning of my career in counter-intelligence -- the process of finding and following what the intelligence services of other countries were doing or trying to do.

My next assignment sent me to Pakistan where both the United States and the Soviet Union were interested and concerned about the Pakistanis' development of a nuclear weapons capability. My job was to find out and monitor how much the Soviets knew about the nuclear bomb project there, as well as how much military assistance they were pouring into Pakistan to help them contain and influence the Afghans. However, like the United States, the Soviet

Union was also interested in maintaining a balance of power between Pakistan and India. At least we had that in common with them during the Cold War.

My work in Pakistan earned me another promotion and a two-year assignment back in headquarters at Langley. Neither I nor any of my close colleagues ever relished stateside assignments, although that's where the bureaucratic wheeling and dealing went on, and where the outstanding agents were said to be labeled if they had the potential for the top CIA positions. However, it never worked that way for me. I detested Washington assignments; it was the excitement of operations in the field that had attracted me to the Agency in the first place. Furthermore, when stateside we didn't get half the benefits we got working abroad. Overseas we received numerous allowances that boosted our modest government salaries considerably: housing allowance, education allowance, cost-of-living differential, and up to 25% supplemental pay for hazardous duty or unhealthful climate conditions. In most assignments abroad our effective pay was, in real terms with allowances, almost doubled.

The truth is that I needed the money. On the advice of a college classmate who became a stockbroker, I had made some bad investments and lost a lot. At least that taught me to be careful in relying on other people.

By now I had been with the Agency almost ten years, and had not yet been able to fulfill my hope of getting back to the Soviet Union on assignment. Checking on Soviet activities around the world was not the same as being in Moscow or Kiev or Odessa, although my present job of studying and analyzing Soviet intelligence efforts in the United States and following the activities and careers of individual Soviet agents did keep me pretty busy. And I must also confess I was still unhappy with my financial condition.

And that is how things were when I met a man at the English Speaking Union in Washington, sort of a club where a few Englishmen and a motley of foreigners used to meet and drink and try to impress each other with the fact that they could speak English or knew a few English words. I met a Russian there that I found interesting, Vladimir Petrowsky, who was in Washington on matters of financial dealings with the International Monetary Fund. At least that's what he said. He liked talking Russian with me, and I liked playing chess with him, but right from the beginning I felt that he knew more, and WAS more, than he let on.

I later learned that Vladimir was working through the Soviet Embassy and that he was an agent of the KGB, which of course is their equivalent of our CIA. He also seemed to know more about me than I would have expected, such as the fact that I worked for the US Government and where. He also knew something of my financial situation, for he offered me a significant amount of money to find out a certain little piece of information for him regarding the amount of foreign aid we were furnishing India and Pakistan. The information he wanted wasn't even classified. Heck, I thought, no law against this. So I got it for him, got paid, and had no sense of guilt in having done anything wrong. But that was the start of something bigger.

It was quite a long time before I was able to identify Vladimir as an employee or officer of the Soviet Embassy; he of course was using an alias, but a little later he gave me another job which was to find out whether a certain Soviet agent was passing documents or information to insurgents in Guatemala. Now, that was my meat; my job was knowing about Soviet agents and their activities. In the course of my regular work at the CIA, I had followed the paper trails of Soviet agents all around the world, and in some cases I had even made trips to Prague, Vienna, Istanbul, New Delhi, Cairo, and other places where the Soviet espionage system was most active.

It is hard to say whether the information Vladimir was asking for this time would have been considered classified. While I will always take risks when there is good reason to do so, I don't like taking risks when it's not necessary. So to cover myself I went to my boss, William Graver, Head of the European Division, to tell him what I was doing, stressing how this contact might be valuable to us at the CIA. He gave me the green light, plus a few tidbits of information I could pass along to encourage the connection without jeopardizing the security of the United States too severely.

My relationship with Vladimir continued to strengthen until one day he told me he had a "friend" who wanted to have lunch with me. It turned out that the friend knew almost as much about my work at the CIA and about my earlier life in Russia as I knew myself. He said he was impressed with the record I had left as a leader of my section of the Youth Group back then, and "knew" I was sympathetic to the goals and aspirations of the Soviet people. He was a high-level recruiter for the KGB and thanked me for the modest services I had provided his government recently. Then he offered to put me on an annual salary, or "retainer" as he called it, simply to pass along certain other bits of information that would probably be unclassified or in any case not important enough to weaken US security or cause any worry to the US government. He enhanced my sympathies toward the Soviet Union significantly when he mentioned the figure of my "retainer," which was slightly more than double my present salary from the CIA.

I figured there were a lot of things I could tell the Soviets that might help them understand how things stood in world affairs, without really threatening the security of the United States. So, without mentioning my "retainer," I explained to my boss, Mr. Graver, and to his boss, Mr. Santoni, that I intended to continue developing my contacts within the KGB for the future value they could be to our great nation. Of course, at the same time I was encouraging the confidence the Soviets had in me which, like a windfall, stemmed from my tolerance for regimentation and my supposèd love of the Communist system they believed I had shown as a schoolboy.

Both the USA and the USSR thought they had a good thing in me, while I knew I had a good thing in them, and a salary now over three times what I could have made any other way. I would get a lot of bills and debts paid off, and start sticking some of the green away in a corner for my old age.

154

The interesting thing about my work for the two countries was how it dovetailed. I mean, much of what I was doing was the same thing for each side, namely, following and tracing the movement and activities of their own agents as well as agents of the other side. I made sure that both the USA and the USSR knew, in rough terms, what I was doing. The bureaucracy of each was confused enough to believe that I was solely on its side and working solely to its advantage. This happy and exciting situation went on for several years, during which time I received a couple of awards and commendations from both countries for my patriotism and the notable contributions I was making.

About that time the CIA learned that there was another double agent working for the CIA and the KGB, believed to be a Russian by birth. It seems the agent was particularly involved in investigations of techniques used to obtain or reveal secrets regarding the reprocessing of "spent" uranium from power plants into weapons-grade material. This technique was highly classified on all sides because of the value it would have to rogue countries intent on hiding their nuclear weapons schemes. Spent power-plant fuel was no longer considered a threat by the IAEA and was now getting little public attention beyond that of a few avid environmentalists. However, at the CIA we knew it still possessed a significant potential for being reprocessed and used in the manufacture of nuclear weapons. I too had been interested and involved with matters regarding the production and deployment of nuclear material for peaceful uses as well as for bombs, so I was assigned the task of tracking down and identifying the KGB agent in question.

At that time the matter of sources and disposition of nuclear fuel was also foremost in the minds of the KGB. Only three weeks after the CIA gave me the new assignment, the KGB did essentially the same thing, ordering me to find the flaws in their security system that had allowed a KGB agent to leak valuable information to the enemy.

After several months of search and research that turned into almost two years and covered the world between Vienna, Moscow, Washington, Tel Aviv, Kabul, Islamabad, and New Delhi, I came to the conclusion that the man the CIA had ordered me to find and identify was the very same man that the KGB wanted to apprehend for unauthorized leaking of classified information. I was so delighted with my progress that I patted myself on the back and took a week's holiday to Majorca in the Baleric Islands. I was finally closing in on him!

But there was still work to do. I didn't have him yet. I reviewed all the available information regarding this scoundrel, his work habits, the places he had served, and the people who seemed to be his clandestine contacts. I was constantly astonished at how many of his contacts were my very own contacts as well, and how often he had visited Tel Aviv and New Delhi. And then... a shudder went up my spine when I learned that he too had recently visited Majorca after those other places. At one time he had even assumed one of my aliases, Dr. Stitch. Was he trying to steal my identity? He was a phantom, a ghost, that I had never been able to nail down, and it looked as though he was out to get me! Who's he working for? Who's paying him? These and other thoughts raced through my mind. Is there a price on my own head? I will have to watch myself ever more closely.

I could hardly sleep, and what little sleep I did manage to capture was filled with the most remarkable dreams you can imagine. I dreamed I was falling down a well in a bucket and my unknown adversary was rising in the other bucket with a cackle and an evil *fin* on his ugly *grace*. I dreamed I was in a sword fight with him, separated by a giant pane of glass. He aped my every movement, as though he were my mirror image.

There! That's it! The dream! The dream was the truth! He looked like my image in the dream, and he was my image. It was me. I mean, he was I. I had found the slippery double agent I had been looking for.

I had been chasing myself. Following my own trail, chasing my own tail, as it were.

THE END

Thirty of the Best Short Stories

Happy Thanksgiving

I am a company commander, out here in the boonies where we have been stuck for eight months. Infantry. Some battles, some wounded, some killed, lots of dirt, mud, heat, wet, cold, stink, mosquitoes, leeches, ticks, sores, aches, always on the go, patrols, alerts, keep moving, dragging on, tired, tired, tired. Tired of fighting, tired of the war, tired of this hell hole.

Can't let the troops know how tired I am. Or how hopeless I sometimes feel. Gotta keep their spirits up. When the spirit goes, the man goes. Here since March. Now it's November. Time to think of Thanksgiving. Try to think of something to tell the troops they should be thankful for. The opportunity to serve their country? Worn out. The college tuition the Army will help pay for when they get back to the States? Already used. The fact that they are still alive? That's something we can be thankful for. And our buddies. That's what we are really thankful for, thankful we have buddies. Of course, as Company Commander, I can't afford to let myself get too buddy-buddy with the troops. Could lead to a loss of discipline and respect.

One of my PFC's doesn't seem to have any buddies either. Kid from Alabama, named Joe Billy MacKenzie. It seems as though most of the kids I know from Alabama and places like that have two first names, usually in backwards order from what you would expect. I had a sergeant, Henry

159

John Campbell, from Tennessee, who was killed back in July. Joe Billy had enlisted, although most of the others in my company were drafted. He is pretty much a loner, doesn't talk a lot, keeps his rifle clean and tries to keep his boots shined -- a nearly impossible task out here. I often feel he is watching me, seeing what I do, and sometimes he just follows me around when he has free time.

Joe Billy came from a family of poor sharecroppers. I learned he had no parents and had lived with a deaf aunt who died when Joe Billy was 11 years old. He left the orphanage when he was 16 and tried to join the Army, but of course he was rejected -- too young. He never graduated from high school but began studying toward a GED while working in an auto garage, at first waxing cars then helping with paint and body work, jobs that didn't require much in the way of communication skills. Then he tried to join the Army again, and this time made it. I don't know whether he had to lie about his age to get in; I guess that happens on occasion, but I never investigated it in his case. Anyway, he must have had a pretty miserable childhood.

As I was saying, it was getting on to Thanksgiving. The best the mess sergeant and I could get from the battalion supply officer beyond our usual C rations and K rations and that sort of stuff was 144 miniature cans of potted turkey meat and forty pounds of flour that hadn't gone moldy quite yet, and twelve cases of O'Doul's beer, non-alcoholic. Now, I like a can of beer as much as the next man, but I had no desire whatsoever to get the real thing for the troops, even if I could have done so -- too dangerous with the enemy lurking about, five or ten miles away, or sometimes five or ten yards away.

160

Fortunately we had a couple of men who liked to sing, and, I thought, if I could get them to lead some singing, the boys might forget how pathetic this Thanksgiving was. So after we finished eating the miserable turkey pâté on toast, and downed most of the imitation beer, we started in singing some Thanksgiving songs, like "Now Thank We All Our God," and "We Gather Together," and even "Praise God from Whom All Blessings Flow."

I was proud of my men who took the feeble Thanksgiving effort in good spirits, some of them even with tears in their eyes. Then, just before I was ready to turn in for the evening, PFC Joe Billy MacKenzie came up to me, saluted, and said, "Sir?"

"Yes," I said, "what is it?"

"Sir, this has been the happiest Thanksgiving I've ever had."

THE END

Rewriting History

Out high school history teacher is really weird. I don't mean that he is an odd-ball, or strange, or anything like that, but just weird. Like, he is unique, if that is the word. One of a kind. He does things that I don't think any other history teacher would ever think of. I mean, he gets the class involved in doing things that you would never expect to do in a history class.

For instance, most history teachers and historians will tell you about what happened back in the days of yore, and then they will tell you HOW it happened, and then they will tell you what led up to it, and then give you all the reasons for why it HAD to happen the way it did. They will practically come right out and say it couldn't have happened any differently from the way it DID happen.

Well, Mr. Miller, our history teacher in the eleventh grade, had a different concept. His idea was that the way the history of the world unfolded was to a considerable extent due to chance, or that it was influenced by decisions or whims of individuals in power that could have gone one way or another. Maybe it was to test his theory that he gave us an interesting assignment last fall.

The assignment was to chose and discuss a point in the past where some decision was made or some action taken that could have been different, and could therefore have made a significant change in the subsequent course of history.

163

Most of the class immediately focused on wars, because most of the history we had been getting up to that time consisted of a series of wars, one war after the other, from the Peloponnesian War to the wars in Iraq and Afghanistan. Like most Americans, my class loved wars and the flag and patriotism and all that. But one of my friends wrote about how we could have avoided World War II with Japan if only we had developed the atom bomb three years earlier and dropped it on Tokyo and other cities over there in August 1941 instead of August 1944. Like, preemptive, was the word he used. Another classmate wrote about how neat it would have been if Ontario and Quebec had joined in with the thirteen colonies in 1776 to throw off the British yoke; how they could have killed off some of the British authorities up there, and we would all be one happy country now, Americans and Canadians. And even Jimmy McLaren, my best friend, considered what Europe and the world would look like if the Germans had won World War I, known then as "The Great War." As he saw it, World War II would have been unnecessary because everyone would already have been speaking German, and furthermore the Cold War with the Soviet Union never would have had to happen.

I was a little more realistic, however; I chose a subject that really could have been different. You see, I was interested in the Civil War, right here in the United States, where more people died than in all the other wars the United States has ever fought in, over the years and decades, including the Revolutionary War, the War of 1812, the Seminole Indian War, the Mexican War, the Spanish-American War, World War I, World War II, the Korean War, the Vietnam War, the Granada War, the Panama War, the

164

Iraq War, and the Afghanistan War, and any others I may have left out, including the War of the Twin Towers.

When Abraham Lincoln was inaugurated in March, 1861, the country was in a turmoil that, some would contend, was at least partly his own fault. The subject of my paper for the class was how the course of history would have been changed if Lincoln had taken a different approach to the problematic situation confronting him at the time he was sworn in to the presidency.

This is what I believe Lincoln could have said in his First Inaugural Address. Of course, I used a lot of the same words and phrases that Lincoln used, just changing the important parts. Here is what I came up with and submitted to Mr. Miller:

-        -   -

LINCOLN'S FIRST INAUGURAL ADDRESS,
(Mar 4, 1861)
REVISED VERSION

by Jimmy O'Toole

"Fellow citizens of the United States:

"In compliance with a custom as old as the government itself, I appear before you to address you briefly, and to take, in your presence, the oath prescribed by the Constitution of the United States, to be taken by the President before he enters on the execution of his office.

165

"I do not consider it necessary, at present, for me to discuss those matters of administration about which there is no special anxiety, or excitement.

"However, I do want to announce that I consider that we -- the Republican Party and I, and indeed, all lovers of freedom in these United States -- have won the long struggle in which we have been engaged, regarding the question of Slavery in the Territories. Soon there will be no more slavery in the Territories belonging to or constituting part of the United States now or in the future.

"For reasons and purposes which I believe are as much political as economic, the position of the those persons of influence in the Southern States has for over twenty years called for the opening of some, if not all, of the Territories to slavery. As you know, and as I have publicly stated on numerous occasions, I do not have, and have never had, any intention of attempting to change the status quo of slavery in those States in which slavery presently exists. While in my heart I believe that slavery is morally and ethically wrong and that it is an abomination on the character and soul of any man who professes to love democracy, nevertheless I acknowledge that the presence of slavery, in those States in which it already exists, is recognized by the Constitution of the United States, which I have sworn to uphold and to defend. But that Constitution does not extend to the Territories. You also know that it has been my staunch position for many years, and was the platform of the Republican Party which last November elected me to be the next President, that slavery must not be allowed to extend into the Territories.

"The State of South Carolina and six other States have officially announced that they have seceded from the Union, and are apparently forming their own union, or Confederacy. Other Southern slave-holding States may also secede and join them in the proximate future. I bear no ill will nor malice toward them. I regret that they have made this decision; they contend that their economy and society have grown so different from the direction in which the North has evolved that they feel they have no other choice. However, the practical effect of their secession is to remove the slavery question from the Territories and from Territorial Governments, and, I sincerely hope and expect, from future States to be formed from Territories seeking admission into the Union. Henceforth, all present and future Territories of the United States, shall be free of slavery.

"Within the next few days I shall issue orders for Federal forces to evacuate all military establishments which we still garrison in South Carolina and those other States which have already seceded or which may decide to secede. Other Federal activities such as the mail, law-enforcement, tax-collection, conscription, maintenance of roads, railroads, canals and other public works, will be phased out in an orderly fashion as local operatives assume responsibility for these activities. Citizens of any State which has seceded shall no longer be considered Citizens of the United States unless they shall have made a statement of intention and taken an oath of allegiance within one year of the secession of that State. My Cabinet officers and other officials will be meeting with designated officials of the seceded States or their representatives in the Confederacy in order to work out equitable financial compensation and division of commonly held property as well as appropriately proportionate assumption of the national debt and other responsibilities and obligations. I expect trade relations between the two countries to continue essentially as they have been among the States in the past, on the basis of 'Most-Favored-Nation' commitments at the very least.

"The Constitution makes provision for the admission of new States into the Union but does not address the question of the possible withdrawal of a State or States. In the absence of specific provisions on the matter, I feel I must accept the fact that powers which the Constitution does not delegate to the Federal authority, or which it does not mention, are reserved to the States, including the power of secession. While I do not believe that the entry of a State into, or its departure from, the United States should be taken lightly, I would not oppose consideration of the readmission into the Union of any or all of the seceded states at some appropriate time in the future should conditions change and so warrant. It is also my fervent hope that those Slave States remaining in the Union will in the relatively near future take it upon themselves to abolish this abhorrent custom, as has been done already in many of the civilized nations of the Western World, although I have pledged not to interfere or attempt in any way whatsoever to accelerate or retard their efforts in this direction.

"Without the Southern States, the North alone still comprises a greater area and greater number of states than the thirteen that originally constituted the United States of America, and it has a population almost four times that of the original thirteen colonies at the time of the Declaration of Independence. While the secession of the Cotton States may weaken the economy of both the North and the South, I nevertheless intend to dedicate my administration to the maintenance of good diplomatic relations and all possible social, cultural, and economic ties with our cousins to the south, even if we no longer call them brothers. Our government may have been weakened, but it has not been destroyed. We have vast new Territories in the West and the Southwest recently acquired from Mexico which we Northerners, unhampered, can now develop freely and settle as rapidly as we desire, without the albatross around our necks of political debate over the slavery question that has torn apart our Congress and our people now for decades. While this is not the outcome I would have preferred had I the power to exert my will without opposition, I am convinced that it is the best practical solution to the major problem that has disrupted almost our entire lives and has threatened the lives of countless citizens of this continent of all political and ethical persuasions. I hate war, the thought of war, and the present threat of the worst war man may ever have known. Those among us who call for war do not know the potential horrors of such a war, or what devastation such a war between brother and brother could wreak upon this continent.

"Many of our grandfathers regretted that Canada did not choose to seek independence from entangling European ties and join with us at the time of our own Revolutionary War. Now Canada, although still under British dominion, is virtually an independent nation with whom we are proud to maintain superior international relations in economics and politics, in spite of our differences. I have every reason to believe that our ties with Canada will continue to grow and strengthen.

"Also, with your help, I shall do all in my power to maintain similarly strong and healthy relations with the new nation to our southern borders, the Confederate States of America. We are not enemies, but friends. We must not be enemies. We share common blood and heritage, if not always a common ideology. The mystic chords of memory, stretching from every battlefield, and patriotic grave, to every living heart and hearthstone, all over this broad land, will yet swell the chorus of our brotherhood, when again touched, as surely they will be, by the better angels of our nature."

A. Lincoln

\-   -   -

Our teacher, Mr. Miller, complimented me with faint praise, saying my piece was well written, but that he would have to give me an "F" because it was "un-American." If the higher-ups in the office of the County Superintendent of Schools ever found out he was giving an "A" or even a "B" to such heresy, he could lose his job.

So, that is the end.

THE END

Holy Cow !

They used to call them call-girls. And then it was masseurs, or masseuses. But back when I was growing up they were called prostitutes or simply whores. Not that I ever knew any. I had what I suppose was a lower-middle-class upbringing, although I didn't know that. People never know what they are getting while they are getting it. That knowledge doesn't come until later.

I went to a Catholic school in downtown Providence, but I never really believed all that Jesus stuff. And while I went through the motions of being a good little boy most of the time, I got kicked out and had to go to public school because I wouldn't believe a lot of what the Bible said, and opened my mouth when I shouldn't have. But I guess I got something of a Catholic foundation, for I certainly never would have paid a professional woman for sex. Besides, by the time I was a teen-ager in the tenth grade there were more than enough amateurs in our high school and in our neighborhood to accommodate the urges of any of the red-blooded chaps who were venturesome in that direction, which only included me on rare occasions. Most of the guys were more talk than deed anyway.

Nobody in my family had ever been to college, as we didn't have much money, so after I got out of high school I got a job with the Mayflower Moving Company and got married soon after that.

171

I've been married twenty-one years now, and have always been faithful to my wife. At least, up to now. She is good looking and romantic, and I never met anybody I liked better than her. Probably the worst that I could say about our marriage is that it got a little boring at times. I won't say I never got any ideas from looking at other woman now and then, but I guess I never had both the courage and the opportunity at the same time to do anything about it. But something happened one weekend in Fort Lauderdale, Florida, just north of Miami. I don't know why.

I was still working for Mayflower, where I have been since before I was married. My wife and I have a tall, slim, red-headed daughter named Dilette, who I admit has always been the apple of my eye. She is our only child now, since her younger brother died in a street fight in downtown Providence two years ago. Dilette was a name my wife and I concocted ourselves; we thought it smacked of our French and Italian heritage and liked the sound of it.

I wanted Dilette to go to Brown, where she would be close to us. I had saved up almost $30,000 toward her college education. It had been a dream of mine to see one of my children go through college; it would be almost as though I myself were going to college by proxy.

But she never liked the Rhode Island climate very much. However, she did like swimming and the ocean, and darned if she didn't somehow get herself a scholarship to the University of Miami, on the swimming team. She was happy with her life there, and used to write home jokingly saying that things were "going swimmingly" for her.

By now I was regional manger of the Trucking Department of Mayflower's Eastern Division, and a lot of my work was done in the office, on computers. By February of Dilette's freshman year, while we were still in the middle of Rhode Island's nasty winter weather, the idea hit me of moving to Florida myself. Mayflower had an office in Miami which I should be able to use for my own operations. With most of my work being done on computers, I probably could have worked almost anywhere. I decided I should fly down to Miami for a couple of days to check out the possibilities and make some inquiries.

My birthday weekend was coming up, and I had already planned to take a few days off and fly with my wife to Bermuda to celebrate. However, she came down with a bad cold and said we should cancel the trip and maybe do it another time. She was glad to agree I should take that weekend to go to Miami, as that would be much more important in the long run anyway.

So I did it. I left Providence Airport Thursday morning for Miami, took a taxi over to the Miami Sands Hotel, and spent the next forty-eight hours checking out the Mayflower office premises and local facilities. I soon concluded that it wasn't going to be too difficult for me to get my place of work switched from Providence to Miami. I would be covering the same Eastern sector of the United States, using the same computers as before, and practically the same office furniture. My wife was always amenable to most of my suggestions, and I didn't expect any objection on her part to our making the move to Florida.

I certainly wanted to see Dilette for dinner, or lunch at least, while I was there: I called the number at her dorm Friday afternoon and a couple of times Saturday morning, with no luck. I left my hotel number on her answering machine, but she never called back. Oh well, she is a busy girl, never easy to get a hold of.

By five-thirty Saturday afternoon I had found out all I wanted to know about the job. I hadn't had any lunch, so I stopped off at a little steak house for an early supper, and then went on back to the hotel. I took off my tie and put on a short-sleeve print shirt so as to look as though I were in Miami for fun, and went downstairs to check out the hotel bar.

Now came sort of a surprise, for there, sitting at the bar watching the Florida State -- Georgia Tech football game, I recognized a vaguely familiar face. On closer inspection, it turned out to be that of an old high-school classmate of mine, Jimmy Hardweiler, whom I had not seen in 25 years. I remembered that in high school he was always one of the Big Men On Campus and an athlete. He also had a reputation of being something of a cut-up and the nemesis of the nuns who were our teachers. It turned out that he was now a lawyer living in Sarasota, and he too was in Miami for a couple of days on business. To tell you the truth, I was a little surprised that he still knew me after all these years.

We did some perfunctory back-slapping and I had a couple of whisky sodas while he was finishing his beer and having another. By that time the football game was over, so he up and said, "Are you alone?"

"I'm alone now; my wife's back home in Providence. Why?"

"What are you doing this evening?"

"Nothing. Maybe go to a movie or something."

"Wanna go to Fort Lauderdale?"

"Why would I want to go to Fort Lauderdale?"

"It's where the action is."

"Action?"

"Yes, action. Wine, women, and song; know what I mean?"

"There's plenty of that kind of action right here in Miami, if that's what you want," said I, picking up on his drift.

"I know some special people in Fort Lauderdale, so that's where I'm staying. At the Regent Hotel. I always stay there when I am around here."

"People? You have plans for the evening?"

"Man, I make my plans as I go, but I know some women there who will knock your socks off, if you know what I mean. Best looking women this side of Dallas, Texas. Come on, have a look. You might see something you like. You can even stay over if you like; there's plenty of room."

Well, like I said, I don't know what got into me. I guess I was feeling euphoric having favorably settled my business affairs, and was relaxed after my scotch and sodas. And beside, I was a little bit curious, so I said, "Okay, why not."

So we went on up to Fort Lauderdale in Jimmy's car, with Jimmy driving and making two or three calls on his cell phone, something that really makes me nervous. Use of cell phones while driving should be illegal, and is, actually, in some places. Should be everywhere. But Jimmy laughed it off. And so I did too, feeling no pain, as it were. He showed me around downtown Fort Lauderdale, which I must admit was a lot more of a city than the sleepy Florida seaside town it used to be. We checked out the port, saw the giant cruise ships at dock, and visited a couple more waterside bars about the time that the effect of the scotch and sodas from Miami was beginning to wear off.

After a while, Jimmy looked at his watch and said, "Let's go on back to the hotel; I want to show you my place. I think you'll like it."

His hotel room turned out to be quite a spread. It must have been the Presidential Suite, with an L-shaped combination living room/dining room, couches, giant TV console, well-stocked wet bar across one side of the room, separate kitchen, and two bedrooms. The hi-fi was playing gently with some soft rock music that he had turned on from his remote when we were coming up in the elevator. I couldn't help thinking that maybe I should have studied law and become a lawyer. Jimmy and his law practice were obviously doing very well.

Well, this is it," he said opening the door. "Come on in and make yourself a drink. They'll be along in a few minutes."

"They? Who's 'they'?"

"The girls, who'd you think?"

"The girls? What girls?"

"Nice girls. Very pretty, very clean. Nice young things."

"How did you know them?"

"I don't really know them. Not yet, anyway. But I know where they come from, and I know that they are all right. I know their manager. They are all beauties, and great fun. You'll see."

You must be thinking I am really dumb, and you wouldn't be far from the truth. It took me until now to finally realize that what Jimmy had in mind was a couple of whores to liven up our evening, or call-girls as he would have said. Well, I was in no pain, and I still had some of the normal urges of a normal man, so I began to look at the coming events with a degree of interest, even budding excitement.

We made a couple of drinks and were about halfway through them when there came a knock on the door. Jimmy went over to open it; I, with great curiosity, was standing right behind him.

"Hi there, boys! I'm Candi. Sorry I'm late."

Well, let me tell you, this Candi was a real looker. A real looker of a hooker. But she was all alone.

"Where's the other girl? There were supposed to be two of you," Jimmy declared.

"Dilette...? She had to stop off at the Ladies' Room. She'll be along in a minute."

"Dilette? That's an unusual name," said Jimmy.

"Yes," agreed Candi. "I've never heard it before. She's a beautiful red-head. You'll love her."

Dilette? Red-head? Holy Cow! What am I hearing? I had to grab the edge of the door to keep from falling. I never thought anything like this would ever happen. What is this world coming to? Wasn't I giving her enough allowance, or what? My own daughter, my dear Dilette! Oh, dear Lord! Holy Cow!

What to do. I had to get out of there, but quick. I slapped my hand against my forehead as though I had just remembered something important, and told Jimmy and his feminine friend that I had an appointment in Miami that I had forgotten about. I knew they wouldn't swallow that, but I couldn't care less. I had to get out of there, that's all. Fast.

I flew back to Providence Sunday morning and got back to the house in the early afternoon. You won't believe this, but, as I opened the door and came into the living room, there was Dilette with a suitcase in her hand, getting ready to leave.   She had been home since Thursday night, having come to Rhode Island for the weekend to surprise me for my birthday.

She gave me a hug and said, "Sorry I missed you, Dad; Happy Birthday anyway.   But now I have to leave on the 5:15 plane to Miami as I've got classes in the morning."

THE END

Thirty of the Best Short Stories

It Was the Best of Times

When I was in high school one of the things we had to do was memorize the opening words of a novel by Charles Dickens called A TALE OF TWO CITIES. "It was the best of times... etc." Of course, it's one of the most famous openings of any novel; maybe you had to learn it too.

Then our English teacher got the bright idea of having us each write a composition about a time in history when we would have liked to live. It was to be an "interdisciplinary approach," mixing History and English, and of course our history teacher thought it was a fine idea too. Cross-cultural understanding, interdepartmental cooperation -- that sort of thing.

Most of the guys chose periods of war and conflict where they pictured themselves as heroic warriors, fighting to stem the tide of infidels encroaching on Christianity, or fighting for national independence and separation from tyrannical British overlords or aggressive Yankees, or fighting to save the world for Democracy, or just fighting for the fun of testing out new weapons and techniques. Fighting, fighting. Ugh. Is all that fighting just in guys' genes, or what?

The rest of us, we girls, that is, chose more romantic settings, for the most part. I thought that the courtly life of the sixteenth century in Europe sounded delightful and fascinating, beautiful and romantic, filled with the elegance of gorgeous castles, and royal balls and garden parties, and

181

lovely décolleté dresses with diamond necklaces, and handsome princes on white horses, and unsullied nature without a lot of concrete and urban sprawl and noise and pollution everywhere. So I went back to the library and did some research about the time and place I had chosen to be my ideal.

I looked up chivalry and gallantry, and lugubrious and adamantine and lots of other medieval words. Chivalry really means how you ride a horse, and gallantry refers to your boyfriends or lovers, if you are a woman. Gallant means taking care of a lady, and opening the doors for her, and paying her bills, and things like that. I think I would be happy with a few gallant men around me. One or two, at least. Adamantine means staying faithful to your boyfriend when he is off on a crusade. I'm not sure I could be adamantine -- I'm really an awfully sweet person.

I came across a lot of wonderful, mysterious-sounding, dirty words, like aphoristic, corpulent, formulate, lucubration, and redolent. And the gallivanting gentlemen who were always ready to pick up a lady's hanky, or panky, or both. I may not know what all those expressions mean, but I do know they must mean exciting things, for I get excited just reading words like that, especially when I read them aloud to myself in my room after I am supposed to have gone to bed. It all sounded so beautiful and romantic.

I read about one Scottish King who particularly attracted me, named James. He was only one year old when he became king on the death of his father, James IV, in 1513. So that made him King James V. However, because of his young age, they let his mother, Margaret Tudor, stay on and help him govern for a while. She was called a regent. Of course, people often died young in those days, so it was always a good idea for you to get started on your career early in life. Since James had to be ready to take over the responsibility of governing by the time he was 21 at the latest, all his friends and relatives helped groom him for the job. He was able to develop many outstanding talents and all the proper social graces, as well as useful contacts with important people everywhere. He was a likeable young man, good looking, strong, a fine horseman, and, naturally, rich. Just the kind of person I myself could fall in love with. I must say the idea was very beautiful and romantic.

I think I was in love with James just reading about him. He was rather carefree, chivalrous toward the ladies, fun-loving, and athletic with the other young gentlemen of the royal court. He even wrote poetry when he had time between jousting events and various other athletic contests. It all sounded so beautiful and romantic.

The women who belonged to the Queen's entourage of ladies-in-waiting all adored James, as I would have too, had I been there. However, since he had grown up with them and knew them almost as though they were his sisters, when he was 24 and the time came for him to look around for a wife to fill out his life and help him plan for future generations, he cast his eye farther afield. Now France had a reputation of producing lovely nubile maidens, many of whom had learned to speak fluent French, which was of course the favored language of the upper classes throughout Europe and the rest of the civilized world. A number of James's relatives and ancestors had sampled this supply of beautiful women, and often had even married some of them. It all sounded so beautiful and romantic.

James had heard reports about the charm and beauty and amiability of one particular French damsel named Marie de Bourbon. She was a young lady of proper upbringing and station in life, being the daughter of the Duke de Vendôme, who lived near Lyon, in eastern France, where the royal French court frequently used to go for summer vacation. James was so impressed by the tales he had heard of her charm and wit that he sent two young knights that were friends of his, Archibald and Ethan, over to the Continent to see this remarkable creature and find out whether what he had heard about her was really true. It all sounded so beautiful and romantic.

The two young men returned bubbling over with excitement, and submitted a most positive report to the king. Marie de Bourbon was one of the most beautiful things imaginable. She was also lots of fun to be with; everybody said so. The two emissaries described her with such adulation and intense passion that for a moment James even wondered whether they might have gotten to know her better than they should have. But still, he had the answer he wanted, and forthwith began to make plans. With a wry smile he boldly announced, "I will go forth to France to see this remarkable beauty that has come to pass; I shall make her my bride and we shall live happily ever after and have lots of children." It all sounded so beautiful and romantic.

Now for a Scottish king to marry the daughter of a French Duke, protocol required his going through channels, and channels meant not only the English Channel, but also François I, the King of France himself. Proper approval would be required, and a meeting would have to be set up to introduce the happy couple to each other. So, trusting the intimate advice he had received about this Marie de Bourbon, James told his ambassador to France to make the necessary arrangements for a meeting and his introduction to Marie de Bourbon. When that had been taken care of and James received word that the coast was clear, he set off with a suitable entourage of Dukes and Earls and other nobles, including Archibald and Ethan, who now knew the way, to plight his troth to this lovely daughter of the Duke de Vendôme.

It all sounded beautiful and romantic. However, things didn't work out quite as James expected.

After several days wending their way across northern and eastern France, sampling the bread and wine and cheese and *paté de fois gras* as they went, the group set up camp one afternoon on the edge of a lovely, calm river meandering through the woods near Lyon, their destination. Just before sunset they heard the sound of splashing waters and happy young soprano voices wafting across from the far side of the river.

With understandable curiosity, James and the others made their way along the shoreline until they were closer and had a good view of the source of the gaiety. And what a view! A dozen nubile maidens bathing in the late afternoon sunshine, laughing about, as they threw handfuls of water at each other and scrubbed each others' backs with sand and river mud. Now, you must remember that this was in the olden days, before the time of bikinis, or any other bathing suits for that matter. If you wanted to go swimming or wading in the river, you just went in the way

185

you were, and if you didn't want to get your clothes wet you left them on a rock or a tree limb at the riverside, and in you went.

This didn't mean that the girls had no modesty, for when one of them spotted the fellows looking at them from across the river, with broad grins on their faces, she let out a suitable shriek, calling out to the others, "Men, men! There are men over there!"

"Where?" said one of the pretty girls, looking around to see, with understandable interest.

"Oh, my!" bellowed another.

"The rascals!" screamed a third.

"We'd better put on our things," said the wisest and most beautiful one of all, modestly coughing once or twice and covering herself with her hands and elbows as best she could.

Alas, too late. James had already seen her, however briefly, and the graven image of her charms immediately etched itself into his eyes and his mind and heart. James was suddenly in love, heels over head, completely, passionately, hopelessly. It all sounded so beautiful and romantic. But the girls scampered away before James and his followers could find a boatman to take them across the river to follow up on their great find.

It is an understatement to say it, but James was disturbed, not just in the way that all the young men there with him were disturbed that day, but because he now realized he could never really be true in his heart to anyone else but this lovely nymph of the riverside. That meant he could not, in all honesty, and in all chivalry, give his heart in marriage to Marie de Bourbon, the daughter of the Duke de Vendôme, who had doubtless already gotten quite excited upon learning a king was coming to visit and look her over. Oh well, that's life, but it left James in a quandary. He had no way of knowing who the river maiden was who had caught his eye and his heart, and he fell into deep depression. It all sounded so beautiful and romantic.

"Cheer up," Jimmy Boy, said the Earl of Fife, James's best friend. We'll go on to Lyon and meet King François, who will doubtless put on a nice spread for us -- with more good French bread and cheese and maybe some *Châteauneuf du Pape*. There will probably be a few young women there too, and we can still have some fun. We'll just have to make the best of it. You may never forget Psyche the River Nymph entirely, but she doesn't have to dominate the rest of your life."

"I don't know," said James.

He was so in love he could hardly eat. Fortunately though, he could still drink, and luckily all this was happening in the wine country of France. Of course, all of France is wine country, but the region of eastern France is one of the best. It all sounded so beautiful and romantic: he, the young king, falling for a beautiful damsel, and so in love he couldn't eat. Couldn't eat much, anyway. It must have been like when you get pregnant and all you want is yogurt or popcorn or cucumbers.

187

James wasn't convinced, but on reflection realized that the Earl was right and that there wasn't anything else for them to do anyway, so the next day they pushed on to Lyon.

When they got to Lyon, King François gave them a splendid reception. "I want to give you a party tonight," he said, just as the Earl of Fife had predicted. That evening, before the ball, François presented his sons (the two princes) and his daughter (Princess Madeleine), to the visitors. James was suddenly transfixed, unable to believe his eyes, for there before him, in a sumptuous gown, was a beautiful young woman with an uncanny resemblance to the nymph of the river. The lovely lass demurely coughed once or twice and went scarlet with embarrassed modesty, and James promptly realized that this young lady, Princess Madeleine, with the magnificently turned legs and firm, shapely torso pointing up in his direction, was indeed herself the Lady of the River. There was no doubt: she was wearing a gorgeous pale blue satin gown and James recognized her unmistakably from her décolleté neckline. It was all so beautiful and romantic.

James didn't wait long; he knew what he wanted. The next morning he asked François for the hand of his daughter. François agreed forthwith; he liked James and also liked the idea of the implicit alliance with Scotland that such a marriage would bring. François always welcomed allies in his continuing series of wars with the forces of Charles V of Spain, the Holy Roman Emperor, and the thought of a few well-trained Scottish Highlanders with bagpipes coming over the hill at a critical moment was very pleasing to him.

The engagement gave grounds for fêtes that lasted throughout the autumn, and the marriage was celebrated January 1, 1537 at Notre Dame Cathedral in Paris. What could be more romantic? Madeleine, who had always wanted to be a queen, now would see that dream come true. She adored James her new husband, was madly happy. It was all so beautiful and romantic.

Following a lengthy honeymoon, relaxing on the Riviera between San Tropez and Monte Carlo, King James took his bride back to Scotland in May, after the cold winter there had almost ended. He looked forward eagerly to showing her off to his buddies, bragging, as it were, about what he had found and his conquest. Madeleine was delighted at the thought of getting to know another country and its people, and the opportunity to learn the English language so she could begin to understand what her husband was saying when he was alone with her after supper. It was all so beautiful and romantic.

The ladies of the Scottish court lavished their attentions upon her, and the young gallants always hovering about showed uncommon willingness to help her fill her every need or help her in any way. But, tempting though these offers were, the dutiful young wife refrained from yielding to their exhortations. Still, it must be admitted that she enjoyed the attention she aroused in her new country. But it was James she loved. She looked forward to a long and happy life with him and lots of children. Life was idyllic. Couldn't be better. It was all so beautiful and romantic. It was the best of times.

Two months later she was dead.

Thirty of the Best Short Stories

Tuberculosis.

She was seventeen years old.

It was the best of times; it was ...

THE END

Do You Think You Can?

I am a twenty-five-year-old brunette and not bad looking if I do say so myself. I must not be the only one who thinks so, because I have had three and a half offers of marriage already. The half came last month, from my friend Michael Evans. He was about to pop the question when his cell phone rang. It was his mother wanting to know what he was doing out so late. Somehow that cooled things down rather rapidly. Both him and me. But my story is not about Michael; it's about my little brother, Gerôme.

My little brother is a brat. I mean, a real brat. Always has been, ever since he was born.

I was eight years old when he came screaming into the world, maybe as an afterthought. They should have washed him down the drain while they still had time. He was the ugliest, noisiest, smelliest thing you ever saw, but our parents thought that his rear end was made of gold and that he was something Incarnate from Above.

I had had it pretty good up to then, as I had been an only child. I do admit that I had everything I wanted, or if I wanted something I didn't have, I could always get it from Dad by buttering him up and telling him how much I loved him and all that. He was an easy touch.

But that was before Gerôme came into the household. Then it was Gerôme that got all the attention, from Dad and

191

Mother both. I was supposed to show a loving interest in the little monster, and let him bring out my motherly instincts. I have to admit he was kind of cute sometimes, like when I put vinegar in his milk bottle and watched his face screw up when he drank it. That was really funny.

As soon as he started to walk, Mother bought him a tiny wooden truck with a string with a little red wooden ball on the end of it for a handle. Not surprisingly, it was called a pull-toy. He loved it and pulled it along behind him all over the house. We played a game where I would put my foot on the truck and tell him to pull harder. He would tug and tug with all his might. Then I would quickly lift my foot and Gerôme would fall over backwards. He was really funny. Then he would start crying and Mother would call down, "What happened to Gerôme?"

"He fell down," I explained. "He's all right. He just wants attention."

He kept his truck in a box by the side of the bed. Sometimes I would take it out and hide it. He would start bawling, and say, "Where my twuck?"

"You must have left it in the living room," I would say. He would go off looking for it, all over the house, while I was putting it back in its box. Frustrated to the point of fury, he would accuse me of knowing where it was.

"It's probably in its box where you left it." And with that he went and found it and finally quieted down, for a time.

All during the years he was growing up, the thing that always frustrated him the most was my hiding something of his, like some of his soldiers, or his baseball, and later his pocket knife. You wouldn't believe how furious he got; he would jump up and down and his face would get red as a beet. Of course after a while I usually put his things back where they belonged, and said he just wasn't paying attention to what he was doing and wasn't looking carefully. In our arguments I could always get Mother and Dad to side with me.

Through the years I had to keep poking a little fun at Gerôme just to be able to stand his presence. When he was a freshman in high school there was one good trick I played on him; I let it slip to one of his schoolmates that Gerôme was a latent homosexual. Well, you know how it is with rumors. Before long the word was out all over the campus. You see, that was before it was popular for homosexuals to come pouring out of closets everywhere. No, it definitely wasn't chic to be known as a homosexual in those days, when the euphemism "gay" was just beginning to come into use. He would get mad and throw his arms about and tell everyone, "That's a bunch of hooey. I'm not, I'm not, I'm not!" You can't imagine how funny he was. He was really a riot.

I don't know if I told you, but I only live at home part-time now. I have a job that takes me out to California occasionally for several weeks at a stretch. Otherwise I still live at home. In fact, I just came back from San Francisco on Friday after being out there for six months.

Well, you won't believe: Gerôme was trying to grow a moustache! Seventeen years old, and trying to grow a moustache. It was the most ridiculous thing I ever saw, this little smudge of a gray line across his upper lip.

I waited until one evening when we had some guests in for dinner, and then, when the conversation lagged a bit while we were waiting for dessert, I leaned over, pretending to scrutinize him, saying, "You've got a little something gray on your lip." I could feel the dinner guests beginning to chuckle politely, under their breath.

"I'm growing a moustache," he said quietly, with a mixture of pride and embarrassment.

"Do you think you can?" I said with a smirk, expecting a wave of amusement to sweep across the room.

Now, as I said, I am a twenty-five-year-old brunette, and have lovely dark skin with an olive tint from the Italian side of our family.

Then, would you believe the gall, the nerve, the audacity, and the effrontery of this little brat of a younger brother? How could he be so mean, so uncaring, so hurtful and embarrassing to his own sister? He leaned over toward me, as though he were looking at a little fuzz on my own upper lip, and said, in a low voice but just loud enough for all the guests to hear clearly, "If you can I guess I can."

THE END

What's in a Name

My mother died in April, 1982. I wasn't even there. She was home in Houston and I was in New York City, in a school, a so-called "finishing school," that no longer exists. The Finch School. A school for girls, or young women, as we preferred to be called. Actually it was a school designed to make young ladies out of female riff-raff whose families happened to have lots of money. At Finch the up-and-coming could mix and mingle with the already-there in the social world. The *arrivistes* with the *déjà arrivées*.

School was rigid but fun, but not all fun. Not for a girl whose name was Gómez. A Spic, in a Spic-and-Span environment. Sort of like a nigger in the woodpile. Being a Spic was even worse than coming from a single-parent home, which was already beginning to get more and more common by then. I tried to explain to people that Gómez was an old aristocratic name, and that my great-grandfather had been related to Don Valentín Gómez Farías, the vice president of Mexico back in the 1830's and 1840's. But that line didn't work; it did nothing for my social stature. What did work, though, was my mother's gift of half a million dollars to the school for a new wing on the library. After that, when people at Finch spoke to me, they said "Please," and "Thank you," and "Yes, Miss Gómez." And periodically they sent Mother engraved thank-you cards reminding her of the honor Finch had bestowed upon her by accepting her donation.

195

It is interesting what money can do. Like, it can make something out of nothing. Like, a somebody out of a nobody. My mother knew this intuitively, or else had learned it along the way. I found out some things about her -- and me -- after she died, that I had never known before.

I flew back to Houston to help my sister María with the funeral arrangements and a little reception at the church parish hall after the service. I thought it would be a small family affair, with just me and María and María's family -- her husband and two children -- and a few close friends. But in fact there were quite a lot of people at the gathering, many of whom I did not know and had never seen before.

María then insisted that I go right back to New York to complete my year at Finch, saying it "would stand me in good stead." And I did go back, but six weeks later, after finishing, I returned to Houston to be with her once again. (At Finch, you didn't exactly graduate -- you "finished.")

Mother had left us quite a sizeable sum of money in her will, several million dollars in fact. So naturally she was the subject of much of our conversation. Talking to María, I was able to begin piecing together a few things about my mother's life.

Mother wasn't always rich. She was born in Guanajuato, Mexico in 1930 in an old family that had lost everything in the Great Depression that they hadn't already lost in the last Mexican Revolution and the Ejido Land-Reform Program of the twenties. It wasn't only the United States that suffered after the Crash; the whole world suffered, including Mexico. So, just after World War II, as

196

soon as she was old enough to strike out on her own, Mother struck out on her own, and came to the United States. In those days there were no national quotas for immigrants coming to the United States from Western Hemisphere countries. All that anyone needed to come here was good morals (as far as was known), no contagious disease, no intent to overthrow the US government, a clean police record, and the offer of a job in the United States so as not to be "at risk of becoming a public charge."

Mother was very attractive, and came to California to work as a dancer in joint outside of Hollywood when she was still in her teens. The owner of the place had found my mother on a holiday trip to Mexico and offered her the job when he first saw her. Her parents, my grandparents, were apparently happy to have one fewer mouth to feed in their large family. I never knew my grandparents, but I do know that in later years Mom would send money back to them periodically. Of course, there are a lot of people of Mexican ancestry with Hispanic names living in California and Arizona and the rest of the Southwest. Many of them still speak Spanish and most of them did not even immigrate to the United States but are the descendents of people who were already living throughout that vast region when we acquired it from Mexico in 1848, after the Mexican War.

All of this that I am telling you came from what María and I could piece together from our memories, after Mother's death. Of course, most of it came from María, as she was the older one.

197

After my mother had been in California for a while, she began to realize the value of money. She liked dancing in the little shows they put on at the bar, liked the admiring looks and tips she got, which she stuck down the front of her dress, but she was discerning enough to realize these customers were not the cream of society, and her ambition was to rise above her current situation. About that time, a man from Salt Lake City named Brigham Smith was on a trip to Los Angeles when he went out slumming one evening and saw her at the bar. He promptly fell in love with her and took her back to Utah with him. He thereupon borrowed some money to buy her a dance studio and help to set her up in business. She also met other people in Salt Lake City, as we shall see shortly.

Now, Salt Lake City is Mormon country, and Mormons have their own ideas about a lot of things; they sometimes hold views that we would consider liberal, and sometimes views that are very conservative. Mormons accept multiple wives of course, but they do not go in much for dancing, especially pole-dancing and bumps and grinds and that sort of thing that I gather my mother was pretty good at in her day. Brigham Smith himself already had three wives, and he also had many friends who had more than one wife. But Mother was able to get along with all of them. She was a "people person," and everybody loved her.

However, Mother was more of a performer than a teacher, and after a couple of years struggling with the dance studio she gave it up and bought a share in a beauty shop where she had been getting her hair done. This must have been in 1950, for it was about the time that María was born. Maybe having the baby gave her an excuse to stop dancing.

The details of the next few years of Mother's life are rather obscure, but she left Salt Lake City for Houston, where she set up her own beauty shop on a quiet street in the old part of town. "Older," I should say, for there are no really old parts of Houston. And there are no zoning laws in Houston either. You can open any establishment anywhere you want to. Mom did much better in Houston, where people were not constrained by the morals of the church quite like they were in Salt Lake City. In Texas lots of ladies painted their faces and dolled themselves up with fancy hairdos and long fingernails. And short skirts and long shoulder straps -- things unheard of among the Mormons. The shop also catered to men clients, and called itself uni-sex or bi-sex or whatever.

The business expanded and started making quite a lot of money. That's when I was born. Mother bought a large house in the suburbs, where I grew up. We had a big yard with trees and swings and a pool, and plenty of servants from as far back as I can remember. Most of them were Hispanic, but the nurse I loved the best was a Swedish woman named Vibeke. She was really more of a mother to me than my own mother was, and I saw her about ten times as much as I ever saw Mom. Mom often had to work evenings and generally slept late in the morning. We also had a cook named Dora, and Teodoro the chief gardener, and others around the place. Most of them had children too, and they were my playmates until I went away to school. Of course, all this was in a single–parent household. In those days, in the 1960's, the single-parent home was just beginning to be common and almost acceptable. "Acceptable" was a word my mother loved, and I can remember her saying we shouldn't do this or that, because it was not "acceptable." "If we did something that wasn't 'acceptable,' what would people think?"

My mother was both proud and ambitious. Proud of the past glory of her forebears, and ambitious to recover glory for herself and her descendants.

Mexicans and other Hispanics will always talk about their pride in being a people of mixed racial origins, especially Spanish and Indian, and will tell you that the present mestizo race has drawn the best from each source. However, they don't usually believe it themselves as individuals; it is just talk. Some call this racial mix creole. A creole may also have some black blood, or Negro as it used to be called, mixed in, as in Louisiana. Originally, however, creole, or *criollo* in Spanish, simply referred to a person born in the New World of European parents or ancestors. Mexicans with a large percentage of Spanish blood, and hence white skins, are particularly proud of their Spanish heritage, and are careful to protect their white skins from too much sunshine.

My mother had the whitest skin you ever saw. It was clear she felt that circumstances had brought her status down below the level of her proper destiny as preordained by her ancestry; her goal in life should be to restore her status to its proper level. Like I said, she took pride in the family tree of her forebears and wanted to be proud of the tree that would follow her in generations to come. What was to follow her was even more important to her than where she was herself.

So when I was six years old, Mother sent me to an acceptable private school, called the Harris County Country Day School. It was where the "nicest" families of Houston sent their children. Later she sent me to the Westover School for Girls in Connecticut. Both of these schools were expensive, as I later learned, but Mother knew the value of money, and it was worth it. And by then she was making pots of the old do-re-mi.

Mother had lots of friends, all kinds, that used to come by the house. Both men and women. Maybe some of them were clients at the beauty shop; some of them might have worked for her. Some of the women were dressed up very fancy like. Some of them called me "Honey," and "Sweetie," and would call each other by those names too. Names we wouldn't dream of using at Westover. Some of the men would bring us presents or take us to the zoo or the rodeo, and some of them said I could call them "Uncle," like Uncle Don, and Uncle Gregory.

The beauty shop grew with its reputation of catering to both genders; it seems that as many men frequented the establishment as women, if not more. It is clear that my mother's work brought happiness and pleasure to a lot of people.

When I was old enough to notice the difference between one-parent families and two-parent families, I tried asking Mother about my own father. I always got vague or ambiguous responses, like "I'd rather not talk about that now." Or, "Your father left us when you were very young," or, "Your father died in the war."

"What war, Mommie?" I would ask.

"Whatever war we were fighting then. Maybe the Vietnam War. When you were a baby. War is a horrible thing. Thousands of our finest men dying out there, including many of my friends." And María got the same answer, although her father "probably died in the Korean War," when María was a baby.

And we would have to let it go at that. But after Mom had been put to rest and the tiresome process of probate and the settling of the estate had been taken care of, María and I felt we needed some escape and a change of scenery, so we decided that a month on a cruise ship to South America was called for. Neither of us had ever been out of the country before, so we had to get passports, and that meant getting our birth certificates in order. Fortunately Mom was pretty well organized. Her money files, her investments and bank accounts, and family papers like birth certificates, we found in clearly labeled folders. Both of our birth certificates were there, María's and mine, and one baptismal certificate, María's.

"I didn't know you were ever baptized," I said.

"Oh, yes," she said, "and you were too. Mom was a Catholic, you know. That is, before she had her falling-out with the Church. Or rather, before they had their falling-out with her. It seems they didn't approve of her -- I don't know exactly why. Probably because she didn't accept a lot of the stuff the Church believed and taught. She explained it all to me one night a long time ago after she had had a couple of drinks. I don't think she ever intended to tell us all these things."

I looked at the birth certificates. They were very simple and clear. One said María Gómez, female, date and place of birth, and then the mother's name. Mine was similar; it had my name, Blanca Gómez.

Then out of curiosity I picked up María's baptismal certificate, and was rather surprised to see her name given as María Smith Fuentes Gómez. "Where does all this 'Smith Fuentes' stuff come from?" I asked. "It's on your baptismal certificate but not on your birth certificate. Do you know anything about it?"

"Yes, Mother explained that to me too. I never told you this, but when she lived in Salt Lake City, where I was born, she had two husbands. Not one after the other like most people have, but both at the same time. Among the Mormons, men could have two or more wives, so Mom saw nothing wrong with a woman having two husbands, Brigham Smith and José Fuentes. She told me she was deeply in love with both of them, although they were quite different from each other. But she couldn't legally marry the two of them at the same time, so she kept the name Gómez. And since she didn't know which of her two husbands was my biological father, she gave me both of their names, Smith and Fuentes."

"And then what happened?" I asked.

"I think that, later on, the other wives must have gotten jealous of Mother's good looks and ostracized her, and that's when she moved to Houston. Maybe both husbands did die in Korea or Vietnam for all I know; that's what she used to say. But that was before you were born, and I was still pretty little. I don't really remember either of them, and she never talked about them anymore."

So, in that way María helped clarify some things for me, although I could never understand how Mother was able to amass such a fortune by merely running a beauty shop. Had she been playing the ponies, or what? I could only guess. Then I remembered something María had said:

"Did you say I was baptized too?"

"Yes, but that was here in Houston, of course," María replied.

"Do you know where?"

"It was probably the Church of the Immaculate Conception, on Crockett Street," she said.

"I wonder what happened to my baptismal certificate; I would like to see it."

"The church should have the record in their books."

So we went to the church, and, after a bit of digging, the sacristan found this entry; there I was:

June 16, 1962: Holy baptism of

Blanca Gonzales Jones Erickson Martínez Peurifoy Jimmy Espósito Gómez.

Yes, that was me. Gómez was my mother's name.

THE END

Uncle Charlie

Surprises come from strange corners sometimes. Sometimes you think you know people and then find out you don't. Or maybe you DO know them and it is other people that don't know them. Anyhow, one way or another, people will often surprise you.

The surprise came to me just after I got back to the States after spending my Junior Year in France on an exchange program. My boyfriend from my sophomore year, or to be exact, my would-be boyfriend, Jimmy MacMasters, had met me at the airport and was driving me back home when the surprise came.

"Have you heard the news?" he asked.

"What news?"

"About old Mr. Morgan."

"What about him?"

"He's in jail."

"In jail?" I muttered.

"Yes, in jail. Although they'll probably be moving him to the state penitentiary before long. They got him last week."

207

Well, this really came as a shock to me. I was stunned. Speechless. I couldn't believe it. Let me tell you why it hit me so hard. But first, I need to back up a little.

I grew up in a quiet suburb of Richmond, Virginia, in a small but fairly normal household, where I was an only child. Mom had been a schoolteacher before I was born, and, after I was old enough to start kindergarten, she went back to teaching part time. Budgets were tight then, and the school put as many teachers as possible on part-time status rather than full time, because that way they didn't have to pay for benefits like health insurance and retirement plans. Nevertheless, they often had Mom carrying a full-time teaching load. Dad was an engineer with a company that had quite a few government contracts, so he spent a lot of time in Washington and never got very involved in our local activities.

I had lots of friends, though. We lived in a very friendly neighborhood, with get-togethers and barbecues and even what they called "Gone-with-the Wind" garden parties, where everybody would dress up Southern Style in long dresses or hoop skirts. I mean the girls, anyway.

Some of the parties were at the big Morgan house on the corner. The house had a wonderful backyard and a field with flower gardens and old boxwood hedges in a classical criss-cross design like a maze, where you could play tag or hide-and-seek. We always liked to go to the Morgan place because the backyard was so much fun.

Old Mr. Morgan was a lot of fun too. He was always thinking of games for the kids to play, like he would get us in a circle for a dodge-ball game using a soccer ball or a beach ball. Children don't play that much anymore, but it was good fun for the little kids. And we played capture the flag, a game Mr. Morgan must have played when he was little, because none of us had ever heard of that either. Nobody but the kids who went to Morgan's knew what these games were, unless they were parents or grandparents who were born before World War II. But they were still fun, and I loved them.

He used to joke about his name, Charles Morgan, saying it sounded as though he were a sailing ship, or a pirate, and he would make pirate noises or sailing ship noises, and then laugh and say it was too bad he had the wrong middle name. He explained that his full name was Charles Robinson Morgan. Then he would put on a big grin and say that if we didn't like to call him Mr. Morgan we could call him Uncle Charlie. He was really funny. And at Hallowe'en he used to dress up real weird like, and pretend he was scaring us when we came to his door trick-or-treating. But he always had lots of goodies for us. Not just candy, but different kinds of fruit, like tangerines and figs or walnuts and pecans. Or oatmeal cookies. He himself especially loved pecans and used to tell us how good they were for us. And then he would give us a little English lesson. "Healthful," he would say. "Oatmeal cookies are healthful. Healthful cookies make for healthy children."

He also got us to play marbles, and sometimes he would get right down on his knees to play with us, in the dirt. He was pretty good at it, but usually lost. I think maybe he just let us win, but he always made it look as though he were trying as hard as he could. He was that kind of a person.

Sometimes, when we were older, and after getting our parents' permission of course, he would take three or four of the neighborhood kids to the zoo or even the circus when it came to town. We also went with him to the art museum a couple of times and to a concert with a real orchestra once. But he especially loved the circus, particularly the high-wire trapeze artists, so they were my favorites too.

It's funny, but most of the other grown-ups thought he was sort of a recluse. He did stay home a lot, it's true. People said that he wrote poetry and that he had published a couple of books, although I have never seen them. The story going around was that he had been married many years before and had had a son and a daughter, but his wife and both children died in an automobile accident only eight years after he was married. He had lived alone ever since then, over thirty-five years. At any rate, he had never married again, as far as anybody knew. I don't know whether his family had ever lived in the big house; I suppose they must have, for it was a lot bigger than what one person needed by himself. Mr. Morgan never talked about his family, and nobody I knew was bold enough to pressure him about it.

I was actually looking forward to seeing him again after my year in France, although I wasn't a kid anymore. After all, I was now seventeen years old and a rising senior in high school. But I still had happy memories of the good times we had had at his place, and with him, over the years. I have never known anybody else quite like Uncle Charlie, before or since.

So you can imagine how surprised and appalled and upset I was when Jimmy told me he was in jail. I didn't know what to say, except to ask what he was in jail for.

"Child molestation," Jimmy replied. "He was charged with five counts of child molestation and child abuse going back over the last twelve years, and was convicted on one of them. On the other four there wasn't enough evidence, they said."

"Child molestation? Mr. Morgan?" I stammered in disbelief.

"That's right. Charles Robinson Morgan, the son-of-a-bitch. He only got fifteen years... Did you know him?"

"Me...?"

"Yes, you... That son-of-a-bitch. Dirty predator. They should have hanged him or given him a life sentence at least... You knew him, didn't you?"

"No, I never knew him."

THE END

Pretty Good English

Have you ever wondered why it's all right to say, "I speak pretty good English," but not all right to say, "I speak English pretty good"? You have to say, "I speak English pretty well."

I asked an English teacher this question once, and she answered, "It sounds better." Ah, yes, the sound. That's what Philip Levine said when he was conducting the New York Philharmonic Orchestra.

I thought back to grade school. I remember being told in the third grade not to say, "Me and Johnny went to camp..." but to say, "Johnny and I went to camp..." I remember that. Maybe it's the only thing I do remember from the third grade. But to tell you the truth, I thought "me and Johnny" sounded all right, if you are only interested in sound.

And then the other question I asked my English-teacher friend was why you can't say, "My aunt came to visit my wife and I." I also told her I had heard President Obama on TV saying, "He married Michèle and I."* My teacher friend told me he shouldn't have said that.

* <u>Presidential Nominee Barack Obama</u>, heard on the "Jim Lehrer TV News Hour," 08/30/08, where Obama was referring to his old friend and pastor, the Reverend Wright.

Then she went on to explain how to tell what's right. With two things, like "my wife and I," versus "my wife and me," the way you tell is to drop the first item and see how it sounds: "Came to visit I"? "Married I"? Those are clearly no-no's. You wouldn't say "came to visit I," because it doesn't sound right. Therefore you shouldn't say "came to visit my wife and I" either.

But, I protested, I have heard people saying other things where that little rule isn't sufficient to tell you the right way to say something. For instance, President Bush was once quoted as saying, "I trust he and his team a lot."** So in this case the rule about dropping the first of two things and seeing what it sounds like wouldn't help.

And I realized that I, perhaps like many other people, had a desire to speak the language correctly, but that we just didn't know how to do it.

I went to the English teacher again, and this time what she said was, "You can always look up grammar in a book, if you want to. Not many people are that interested. We don't teach grammar as a subject anymore."

"But why?" I persisted.

"It might stultify their creativity."

THE END

** <u>President George W. Bush</u>, cited in Bob Woodward's book "The War Within," page 177, where Bush was referring to his National Security Adviser, Stephen J. Hadley.

```
Louis Valois.  Born 1423, Bourges, France, son of King
Charles VII.  Became King Louis XI in 1461.  Died 1483.

Jacques Rocher Grimpé.  Born 1443, Paris, France.  Became
Astrologer to the King in 1466 when 23 years old.  Was 39
years old when Louis XI died in 1483.
```

The Astrologer and the King

Modern governments and presidents are not the first to have conducted national policy with the aid of astrologers or soothsayers. Here's an example from the 15th century. Jacques Rocher Grimpé was Court Astrologer to King Louis XI of France from 1466 until 1475, a period of almost ten years.

Yes, many kings in those days had astrologers, like Jacques. They also had prisons. Jacques knew a little about prisons -- he had been in the infamous Galliard Dungeon for a short while when he was younger, but now he was almost forty at the time of this story, and doing very well. So you can understand how startled and horrified and dismayed he was when one sunny day the County Sheriff and some other energetic authorities came pounding on his door to tell him he had to go back to prison.

"Back to prison? But why?" He babbled.

"Things have changed," came the reply. "We have a new King now."

-        -   -

Jacques had to think fast...

215

But first, let me tell you how he got into this awkward situation.

When he was very young, growing up in Paris, Jacques Grimpé decided he wanted to be a soothsayer or astrologer. As it turned out later, he was one of the happy few who are able to do what they want to do in life, and also make a living at it. Most people who just do what they want to do are either no-good bums or Bohemian artists, or else they are rich people living on inherited money, or nobility and royalty parasitically sponging off the labors and taxes of the poor downtrodden peasantry.

Even as a child and teenager Jacques was interested in people. He was interested in knowing what people were thinking and what they wanted. Everybody has thoughts and everybody wants something, even kings and generals and idiots and imbeciles. Jacques realized that you can learn a lot about people by listening to them and by just looking at them. Maybe he had a special talent for it, but he found he could tell a great deal from a person's face, from the wrinkles in his brow, the way he lifted his eyebrows, and the way he turned the corners of his lips or stroked his ear or chin with his fingers while he talked.

Jacques learned about people's habits and their inner fears and wants. As he grew, these things became more and more obvious to him. As Sherlock Holmes would say in later years, if a man had mud on his boots, he probably had been out walking in the mud. But some people can't even see that. Jacques began to realize that a lot of the forces that determine both the present and the future course of

216

events in people's lives are revealed right there in their faces and body gestures where he could see them just by looking.

When he was still a teenager he could amaze his school friends by telling them about forthcoming examinations, for instance. He could look into the future and tell them that some exam questions were going to be harder than others. He told them they would have to get more answers right than wrong, in order to pass. He could predict that confident students were going to do better than nervous ones. He could also tell which of his friends were falling in love or breaking up with their girlfriends because he read it in their faces. Things like that were all quite clear to him, but the other students thought he was a genius, or a "psychic" or "soothsayer," as some of them said.

Yes, Jacques had an understanding of human nature in general and a sense of people's feelings and aspirations in particular. And, being a garrulous and gregarious fellow (if you know what those words mean), he was quite willing to talk about what he saw coming over the horizon. People then, as now, loved to believe things that smacked of the miraculous or the supernatural, so Jacques's friends and acquaintances generously credited him with having psychic powers and the ability to look into the future.

Jacques reasoned that if people could look up into the sky and see chariots and archers, and dogs and bears, then in their mind's eye they might also be able to see and believe almost anything he fed them. Any hooey at all. People in those days were no different from people today

217

who will believe anything, from impossible supernatural religious miracles to alien UFO's. People and the human race change but little over the centuries.

At first, Jacques didn't know much about professional psychics and soothsayers, but when he thought about these things he realized that being a soothsayer might be an interesting and rewarding career.

Also his admiration and ambition lay upward on the social scale, toward the aristocracy, even in those days when social mobility was a rare and difficult process. And he was determined to get to wherever it was that he was destined to go, by using his brain instead of his muscles. Peasants used their muscles. Not Jacques.

Jacques became very popular by telling people what they already knew or believed, and they loved him for it. "If that's what they believe," figured Jacques, "why should I disabuse them of it? He made a hit every time, and thought, "maybe I can make something of this." That's when he decided once and for all to become a soothsayer. He visited his local library and other libraries in Paris, reading up on the history and techniques of soothsaying. He studied the psychics, the prophets, and the Gypsy fortune tellers through the ages, as well as the history of astrology, ultimately concluding that it was all a bunch of hooey. But he also knew it worked. "I can do that," he said to himself. "I'll bet I can give out hooey as well as any of them. All you have to do is keep a straight face, don't laugh, and tell them what they want to hear."

His opening began during his final year at school. Because he was the best math student in his class, he was chosen to give a talk on a subject he didn't know anything about. It was set up as a colloquium or symposium or something like that. He was supposed to discuss farming problems and the outlook for next fall's grape harvest and the quality of the wine that would be produced. Now, there were farmers and wine growers present at the gathering, and he could see worry and concern in their faces. So in his speech he told them they should be worried and concerned about the forthcoming crop. Of course in his talk he used a lot of big words and beautiful phrases, and put on a very knowledgeable tone to his voice. As it turned out, six months later, at harvest time, would you believe, the wine growers were worried and concerned, as always, but they gave Jacques credit for having special powers to predict the future.

As luck would have it, word of his perspicacious prowess even got to the King's Privy Council, who were still upset about some poor decisions the King had been making recently.

"You should get a new Court Astrologer," they told the King.

"Yes, but who?" said the King.

"We have one in mind," came the reply.

So that is how Jacques Rocher Grimpé, when he was only 23 years old, became Court Astrologer to King Louis XI. It was as easy as that. Needless to say, he was delighted with the appointment. He liked the job. A lot of influence and no responsibility. Ideal. And he liked the official term "Astrologer" better than "Soothsayer." It sounded more scientific. More high-tech.

Now, the King of France in those days, Louis XI, was by nature very unsure of himself. He suffered from a condition that today would be called an inferiority complex. He didn't become King until 1461 when he was already 38 years old and had almost given up on ever making it. Until then he had divided his time between quarreling with his father, King Charles VII, and chasing pretty women around Paris and across the countryside. As one of the local journalists later put it, he left few footprints, and those were mostly in ladies' bedrooms and boudoirs.

When he finally became King, Louis was still unsure of himself. He spent many hours praying on his knees, but was not sure whether prayers at the chapel or at the cathedral would be more effective, so he prayed in both places, alternating back and forth regularly. He covered himself with medals to give himself fortitude, and made the entire royal court, even Dukes and Counts who were his brothers and cousins, bow and scrape and call him "Sire." But still his insecurity dogged him. Like his father, Louis had to have many mistresses to try to convince himself of his manhood and satisfy his need for solace. And, in a further effort to adopt a macho image, he sent out his armies to subdue uppity peasants in Brittany and Burgundy or to confront various coalitions of English, Spanish, and Austrian forces threatening his security and peace of mind.

So he needed an astrologer to help him plan his military strategies and his taxation policies, and face many other decisions. What would the effect of this new tax law be? (Complaints.) How much will this project cost? (Too much.) Will people find out my secrets? (Yes, there are always leaks.) What will happen to my ratings with the populace if I let them know what I am doing? (Down. The more they know, the more your ratings will go down.)

Louis was never sure that his official decisions were the right ones. Or his unofficial decisions either, for that matter. Never sure which Colonel to promote to General, never sure which Chamber Maid to promote to Mistress of the Royal Bedchamber. (If you want to know which Colonels to promote, ask the Majors. If you want to know which Majors to promote, ask the Captains. If you want to know which Chambermaid to promote, ask the Stableboy.)

Things like that. So you can see why Louis needed a good Court Astrologer to rely upon. And when the new Astrologer, Jacques Rocher Grimpé, got installed, Louis consulted with him regularly, right from the start.

Now, Monsieur Jacques was careful never to tell the King directly what to do. For the most part he limited himself to fancy words and phrases that said what the King wanted to hear or already knew. If he was called upon to predict the result of this or that possible course of action, Jacques always made sure his predictions had plenty of ambiguity about them that he could fall back on if necessary. But the King thought he was a wise and useful fellow to have around.

"I never give advice, Sire. I only tell the truth," said Jacques.

For instance, since the King always fell in love with every beautiful woman that caught his eye, Jacques safely predicted that, if he fooled around with one particularly attractive and ambitions courtesan named Marguerite de Sassenage, he would promptly fall in love with her, (everybody did), and she would soon be bossing him around all over the place. Is that what he wanted? So, just as predicted, and not his intention at all, the King did fall in love with Marguerite. Now, the King had loved a lot of women in his time, but didn't much cherish the idea of being IN love, but there it was. Like people who like to drink too much wine but don't like the idea of BEING a drunk. He tried to hold Jacques responsible. Jacques could only say, "I told you so, Sire." But Marguerite gave Louis comfort and solace, as well as a couple of lovely illegitimate daughters, Jeanne and Marie. Although Marguerite was not able to see into the future as Jacques could, she still held King Louis in the palm of her hand, so to speak. Almost as the infamous Agnes Sorel had held Louis's father, Charles VII, in the palm of *her* hand. Anyway, Jacques's position was still secure.

Jacques the Astrologer and Louis the King were a perfect fit for each other. The King had what Jacques wanted. Jacques had what the King needed. And he did well in the job; all Jacques had to do was tell the King what he wanted to hear. And of course keep any predictions ambiguous.

In time, Jacques got a little bolder and was tempted to make a few more predictions. He learned that, if he were wrong, people would often forget by the time the event had come and gone, or else his predictions were ambiguous enough to let him off the hook, like the Greek oracles of old. If he were careful, he could make predictions that were right no matter what the outcome was. He even predicted that the price of salt, like the stock market, would fluctuate. Of course, it did.

Jacques may have gotten a little too sure of himself and perhaps began to feel he really did have some psychic powers to predict the future. He no longer just told the King what he knew the King wanted to hear. He began to give him something more -- some truths -- as he saw them. And as we all know, sometimes it is the truth that hurts. And it hurt the King.

Indeed, one day Jacques really did look into the future, although in this case almost anybody could have done so. But Jacques forgot one of his most important mantras, namely, "Tell them what they want to hear."

It so happened that at that time King Louis's forces were deployed along the eastern front, stemming the threat of aggressive Austrian terrorists. Jacques predicted the King's army would lose the battle. It was all so very clear: outnumbered forces, poor morale, bad positions, unfavorable wind and weather. Even Dr. Watson could have seen the debacle coming. Jacques knew that the King's army, badly situated and commanded by a nobleman general who drank too much and was distracted by his wife's exorbitant spending habits, was doomed to defeat. And he said so.

But that was not what the King wanted to hear.

Four days later King Louis's forces suffered a disastrous defeat as predicted. The angry King had Jacques brought into his throne room, on to the carpet, as it were, and lashed out at him.

"YOU did it! It's YOUR fault! You were the cause of the defeat of my army at Liège!" screamed the King.

"I'm just the messenger, Sire. I bring you messages from the Gods and the Stars who, like yourself, are all powerful and control the universe."

The King was furious, but what to do?

"Look what you did! You made my men die in battle!"

"With all due respect, Sire, I have no power whatsoever to alter the course of events. My meager abilities are limited to seeing what is happening and what will happen."

"I don't believe you," bellowed the King. You are a Witch! Son-of-a-Bitch Witch! Wizard! Warlock... whatever it is... Anyway, you're a Scoundrel...! Guards!

"I'll have you thrown into prison! In this day of infamy, 2,900 of my troops are dead at the hands of those terrorist Austrians, plus my best General and three mediocre Colonels. Gone! You are so smart, and know so much about other people and other people's lives, now tell me, how long do you think YOU are going to live, you rascal?"

"Sire," said Jacques serenely, knitting his brows in pensive fashion and looking off into his crystal ball beyond the horizon, "I shall die exactly one week before you die, Sire. Seven days before you."

"You are just saying that."

"Oh, yes, Sire. I am just saying that. Because it's true. You will see, Sire, that I am right. Or rather, France will see that I am right, because you will be dead and gone."

"I don't believe you! You are a scoundrel and deserve to die."

"Very well, Sire. Anything you say."

"Off with him," screamed the King in fury. "Put him in the Galliard Dungeon."

So that was that.

But the King didn't sleep very well that night. The next morning he sent instructions to the Galliard Prison to give the new prisoner the best non-smoking dungeon room available, and to make sure he stayed warm and dry, and to give him the best choices on the prison menu, including extra helpings of healthful fruit and vegetables, like orange juice and spinach and broccoli -- things with plenty of vitamin C and vitamin A. In the past, many inmates had died at the Galliard of vitamin deficiency and colds and flu caused by bad diet and drafty corridors.

225

Of course, the King didn't want to believe the dire prediction of his own death so closely following the death of this scoundrel. But why take the chance? The King realized it would be best to keep Jacques Rocher Grimpé alive. Yes. No point in taking unnecessary chances. I don't really want him to die, do I? What good would that do? Maybe -- just maybe -- he is right. Better to keep him healthy. But the infamous Galliard did not have a reputation for the longevity of its residents, even those receiving special treatment. Prison life is not healthy -- not healthful either.

So, although he was still quite vexed with this astrologer, just to be safe Louis called his Minister of Special Interior Operations and together they decided what they had to do to assure that the astrologer would live a long long life.

Then they wisely had Jacques taken out of the Galliard Prison and placed under minimum security house arrest in a pleasant, medium-sized chateau outside the town of Rouen. He was given servants to take care of him, and an entry permit to the Royal Forest for free firewood to keep him warm in wintertime. Don't want him dying of a chill. Some people did in those days, you know. And they didn't have Aleve and Vicks Cough Syrup to temper the dark agony of imminent death.

The chateau had only a very small moat and a very small drawbridge, just big enough to keep out the riff-raff, but the household was provided with a full staff including cook, butler, stable-boy, gardener, and two French maids. There was a little chapel right in the chateau where Jacques could have conveniently prayed had he ever wanted to, or even just given thanks. The King's instructions to the Provincial Governor and the County Sheriff were to spare no expense in keeping Sir Jacques healthy and happy. Especially healthy. He would also be wealthy and of course was already wise enough.

You can imagine how delighted Jacques was with his change of fortune. He now had reached the heights of his youthful aspirations. Had it made. Life was A-okay. Life was beautiful. He was practically nobility, living in his own chateau. Aristocracy, anyway. There is a fine line between aristocracy and nobility. You have to be an insider to see the difference, and Jacques was almost an insider himself now.

Jacques found it easy to get accustomed to the soft life. He was especially delighted to find he had a full Social Security pension and a lifetime healthcare plan, all paid for by the Government, or taxpayers, if you will. Further happiness and solace came from the two French maids, especially the Upstairs Maid, a young girl of considerable competence. You could see that she had outstanding talents even when she was bending over to dust the furniture or sweep the floor.

Jacques joined the local hunt club, took violin lessons and art lessons, and got his chateau on the annual Homes Tour sponsored by the Historic Normandy Foundation, a local tradition and institution, although most of those who came through on the tours were descendants of Germanic invaders from the North, who did not understand all of the peculiar institutions in the countries to their southern borders. Jacques was in Seventh Heaven. Who said soothsaying doesn't pay? He had it all.

For a while. For a number of years.

Then one day the County Sheriff came back to Jacques's place bringing along an emissary of the King, none other than Louis's old Minister of Special Interior Operations, with the news that Jacques had to vacate the chateau and go back to the Galliard Dungeon.

"But why? What's up, Doc? -- if you will excuse the expression," asked Jacques in dismay.

"I'm afraid the jig is up, Sir, if you will excuse the expression. We seem to have reached the limit of your cleverness. You know King Louis XI is dead? We have a new King now, Louis XII."

"I have heard some rumors to that effect."

"The new King doesn't feel bound or obligated by policies and arrangements made by the previous administration. And we don't think our poor departed King Louis XI would be happy in his grave if he knew you were living on in luxury like this after he had died and you were supposed to have predeceased him. So I am afraid it's back to the Galliard Prison with you... Sir."

"Just a minute," said Jacques, knitting his brow slightly and doing some fast thinking. Then he took on a very serious countenance and continued:

"I am terribly sorry. I have an apology to make. I meant to tell you: When I didn't die last month and the king did, I knew something was wrong. I opened my eyes and I went back to read the stars again. I soon realized my mistake regarding what they were saying. In actual fact the stars were saying that I will die one week before King Louis XII dies. I'm not very good at math, and I get my numbers mixed up sometimes. Ex Eye looks a lot like Ex Eye Eye. There's only an iota of difference. I'm awfully sorry about that. Do tell the King, for me, won't you?"

THE END

A WORD ABOUT STYLE

A while ago, after I had written about fifty stories, a friend of mine said she liked my style of writing. My own reaction was that I didn't think I had a style, or that if I did I didn't know it. To me the stories are all individual, all different and unrelated, written separately as they pop into my mind.

Usually I conceive of the ending first, and then go back and think of a beginning that seems to work. Finally I fill in the middle and smooth it all out, injecting bits of humor or philosophy or pathos where the opportunities present themselves, and *voilà*, that's it.

So, in asking myself whether I have a "style," I first asked myself what was meant by "style," and my answer was: "general consistencies." Any consistencies in my stories, except perhaps the use of correct grammar and care in the choice of words, were not the product of conscious thought during the writing process, but only what I can see or imagine now, looking back and comparing.

This is what I came up with: these are the aspects or elements that seem to me most common or consistent throughout my stories.

DHD

THE AUTHOR'S STYLE

An introductory paragraph or two. This may give the setting or may give a suggestion of the action or story to follow. Or sometimes it may be a brief glimpse ahead into the story, followed by a flashback that starts at the beginning.

Surprise ending. I like to give many of my stories sort of a twist or surprise at the end. Sometimes it can be foreseen, sometimes not. Sometimes it depends on the perspicacity of the reader.

Fantasy told as reality. Some of my stories are almost entirely true; some are complete fabrications. Most have at least some seed of truth. After all, life is the fundamental source of ideas for all writers. I usually try to make my stories sound as realistic as possible, even if they are ridiculous.

Easy vernacular to give verisimilitude. My language is normally quite plain unless I am trying to add to the humor, or the description of a character or situation, by the use of unusual language.

Irony and sarcasm. Many of my stories are laced with sarcasm. This is perhaps stylistic; I do not think it reflects a particularly sour nature on the part of the writer. The world is filled with hypocrisies that are sometimes best met with a sarcastic approach that may add to the humor.

Narrator in the first person. I have heard it said that it is amateurish to write in the first person, but that is simply the way many of these stories have come to me.

A small amount of dialogue, near the end. It just seems to happen this way. Perhaps dialogue smacks of familiarity between the writer and the reader, or between the reader and the characters. Such familiarity may develop during the body of the story, making a bit of dialogue seem more appropriate nearer the end than at the beginning.

Time and place are generic. Most (but not all) of these stories could take place anytime, anywhere. Most of my occasional stories about war are not specific as to time and place, or even what war or what country we are talking about. If the writer's philosophical views color his stories, I think the greater the generalization, the better.

Goofy people. I write about goofy people, and people that are not too smart. Maybe it makes me feel superior to do so. Maybe the reader sees himself, or enjoys reading about people that are even dumber than he is. Many Americans don't like, and don't trust, people that are too smart. That is why we don't like Presidents who have an IQ over 110.

Victims of circumstances. Many of my subjects are people who are influenced by forces outside their control. The extent to which luck or chance controls our lives, and how people respond, is rich material for story-telling. Luck may bring an ending with a happy surprise, or an unhappy surprise. It's like the ninth inning in baseball.

Daniel H. Daniels
PO Box 1681
Beaufort, SC 29901

September 4, 2010

Other works by the same author

BAKED ALASKA and Other SHORT SHORT STORIES
BAKED ALASKA
HEADS I WIN, TAILS I WIN
STORMY NIGHT
GOOD NEWS
THE LIVE OAK
THE RABBIT
BITCHES ON THE BEACH
HELLO THERE
PLAYING IT COOL
MAKING ARRANGEMENTS
THAT'S OKAY
ANYTHING YOU WANT
GETTING EVEN
HASTA LA VISTA
IT WOULDN'T BE ADVISABLE
A NEW START
THE PRODIGAL CALF
A FEW MORE DAYS
LIKE I SAID, AN ORDINARY GUY
TURKEY IN THE STRAW
JOHN HARVARD FANTOMA
MY BROTHER-IN-LAW IS A JERK
THE MOUSTACHE
MONEY, MONEY, MONEY
THE WORLD OF ART
THE BEARD
BASTILLE DAY – PROVING A POINT
LOCKS OF GOLD
HYPOCRISY, ANYONE ?
YOU TOOK THE WORDS

VERSE TRANSLATIONS OF MOLIÈRE COMEDIES:
Volume One: DON JUAN AND OTHER PLAYS
    "The Imaginary Cuckold"
    "A Doctor in Spite of Himself"
    "Don Juan"
Volume Two: THE MISANTHROPE AND OTHER PLAYS
    "Love is the Best Doctor"
    "A School for Husbands"
    "The Misanthrope"
Volume Three: THE IMAGINARY INVALID AND OTHER PLAYS
    "George Dandin"
    "The Learnèd Ladies"
    "The Imaginary Invalid"

CPSIA information can be obtained at www.ICGtesting.com
Printed in the USA
LVOW110059220512

282724LV00002B/1/P